Finding My Brother's Princess

By

Rachel Jeffries

Lizard Ventures

Scottsdale, Arizona

Lizard Ventures
Scottsdale, Arizona

First Paperback Edition: May 2011 by Lizard Ventures

ISBN 978-0-615-47614-8
Printed in the United States of America

Book design by Rachel Alicia Jeffries

For My Family and Friends

☺ ☺ ☺

Acknowledgements

Hugs to:

I love my family, especially my parents. They're amazing, and they've helped me every step of the way.

Big thanks to my team of stellar editors: my wonderful mom; my splendid Aunt Heidi; my caring friend, Mrs. Horstman; and of course, my superstar dad. Thank you very much for all of your feedback and support. I really appreciate it!

Last, but not least, thanks to all my wonderful friends. My life is better because of you.

☺ ☺ ☺

Finding My

Brother's Princess

Prologue

When Matt Martin and an unknown girl first walked into Tiffany & Co. on a sunny California August day, Emily Westin had trouble believing her eyes. She was 14 years old and swore to all her friends that she was truly Matt's biggest fan. Emily had watched every single episode of *Ignorance is Bliss* and probably read nearly every tabloid article Matt was featured in.

Therefore, Emily knew Matt was a player. Emily realized Matt had commitment issues. She had read about when he and his costar Alexa Kipley first began dating and that they broke up since Matt had found himself more occupied with kissing other girls than focusing on his relationship with Alexa.

Emily was also the first outside Matt's family and close friends to find out that Matt was dating his sister's best friend, Lilly Thomas. She had seen them sitting front row at the Calvin Klein summer fashion show in Hawaii playing tongue gymnastics. She was also the lanky red head who asked him to sign her program after the show while he engaged all the various CK models.

It was fair to say Emily was slightly obsessed with Matt Martin. After joyfully receiving her treasured Matt Martin autograph she had lingered behind to watch him flirt with a striking brunette model. Even though, the whole time as she watched him flirt with the model, she was truly dreaming of a time when she, Emily, would be in the model's place. And a time, where she'd have a body like the model, too. Sadly for Emily, this was the last she found out about Matt's love life because she had to catch a flight home to Ohio, positive she would never see Matt, in person, again.

And now, for whatever crazy reason, she sat on a couch near the front door of the Beverly Hill's Tiffany & Co. watching a frazzled looking Matt Martin buy an engagement ring.

EMILY'S MOBILE TO ALL CONTACTS: OMG CELEB SCANDAL OF THE CENTURY!!!

Part One

Lilly

1. **Meet the Stars**

LILLY'S MOBILE: carolyn, where were u?!

MY MOBILE: so sorry matt and i had a photo shoot, some kind of "the family of the star" type thing

LILLY'S MOBILE: well u owe me BIG time ☹

MY MOBILE: i'll make it up 2 u, want 2 go shopping on friday???

LILLY'S MOBILE: fine. Lilly is out

     I am the worst friend to ever walk the planet. My best friend ever, Lilly Thomas, invited me to this really big horse show and, I know things come up, but this was a HUGE deal for Lilly. She lives for horses; she lives and breathes them. I'm not a horse person, but of course I put on my "I'll-do-anything-for-you face" and said I'd come. Now, I missed it and I'm officially the worst friend ever.

     But, to be honest, when I say I'll make it up to her I mean it. Big time. Well, sure, shopping? You're probably thinking: that's how you make it up to her big time? I'm not actually going to take her to some boring old thrift store filled with polyester crud. Being my friend has major perks. My 19 years old brother happens to be the star of this hit show called *Ignorance is Bliss* (which, by the way, is totally true). His picture is probably hung on the walls of teenage girls across the nation (which is kind of weird to me).

So naturally I get to go to all these big star events. Cool right? While Lilly thinks we're going just "shopping" Saturday; we're actually going to the Calvin Klein fashion show this weekend in Maui, Hawaii. Yes, you heard me right. I'm just going to tell the president of Northwest Airlines that Matt Martin has an emergency and needs to get to Hawaii pronto and *poof*. Lilly and I (with Matt, of course) are on our way to Hawaii. Now who's the best friend ever?

MY MOBILE: how was the shoot?

MATTY'S MOBILE: awesome! in the scene i got to kiss Alexa & u know how i luv her kissing

MY MOBILE: u r so perverted

MY MOBILE: haha jk i know u r but still...

MATTY'S MOBILE: whatever fyi going 2 Maui tomorrow want 2 come??

Wow, how perfectly did that work out? Now I don't have to make up a ridiculous story about Jessica Alba having a party! Karma is definitely working out for me right now.

MY MOBILE: sure ☺

MATTY'S MOBILE: u can bring Lilly even though i know u will anyways

MY MOBILE: it's like u can read my mind!! thx matty

MATTY'S MOBILE: no big

MATTY'S MOBILE: btw don't call me matty...it is soo not manly

MY MOBILE: then i'm going 2 even more ☺

Having a celebrity brother is fantastic. I mean, yeah, like all brothers, they totally enjoy mocking you, but since they're gone at shoots so much they end up being really nice to you most of the time. It's especially great because I get all the celebrity perks without the worries of bad press and paparazzi.

Thousands of girls across the nation would kill to be me and I mean it. Matt has so many over obsessed fans it's kind of scary. Once Matt was walking down the street and this girl who was like 25 ran over and freaking tackled him. Tackled! Now don't get me wrong it was hilarious, but really? Tackling? Talk about abandonment issues. Hee-hee.

Of course having a "teenage heart throb" brother isn't all fun and games. It's like you're in this constant shadow that just gets bigger with how many seasons the show runs. This shadow only diminishes after the show gets cancelled and he ends up desperately begging to be on *The Celebrity Apprentice*.

Even, though I think that would be beyond cool because I haven't missed an episode yet. I just get the impression celebrities do not agree with me, seeing it pays them, like, nothing. And after all, time is money.

My BlackBerry vibrates and I scramble across the room to get it. Last spring, my brother was invited to a BlackBerry event called the "BlackBerry Bash" and Scarlett Johansson won a new BlackBerry Storm, but she didn't want it so she gave it to ME. How cool is that?

ALEXA'S MOBILE: hey girlie! ;p

MY MOBILE: hey! we haven't talked in 4ever!!!

ALEXA'S MOBILE: i know! what r u doing 2nite??

MY MOBILE: nothing

ALEXA'S MOBILE: want 2 go 2 Pepperoni & Co.??

MY MOBILE: yeah!

ALEXA'S MOBILE: pick u up @ 5? ☺

That's Alexa. If you want to go into specifics she's who my brother loves to kiss. Alexa is also a star on *Ignorance is Bliss* and probably my best friend aside from Lilly. She plays beautiful, funny, sweet and endearing Harper who is Daniel's (my brother's character) love interest. Her golden blonde hair is long and has waves a mermaid would kill for. Her eyes are a striking combination of gray and violet and her smile bright and warm. Alexa is what you would call an out of the ordinary beauty.

Alexa and Matt dated for a couple of months, but Matt cheated on her. And, so naturally, I told her. Alexa was devastated! In one episode of *Ignorance is Bliss*, Alexa was supposed to pretend slap Matt, but let me tell you that was no pretend slap! Another time, they were doing a photo shoot for *InTouch* magazine where, for whatever reason, they were supposed to be having a food fight in the photos and Alexa dumped a bucket of Tabasco sauce on Matt's head and it got in his eyes. His eyes burned for hours on end.

I don't think Alexa ever completely forgave Matt, but honestly who can blame her? The boy is a player. He loves girls. To him, they're like "Baskin Robins," he has a different flavor every week.

2. Sweetheart

Alexa pulls up to my family's massive brownstone house in her shiny (probably just waxed) white Porsche 911 Turbo. I totally can't help but envy her. She is so lucky she can drive! I mean, Alexa's 17 (I'm 15) and her first car is a Porsche convertible. How unreal is that?

"I'm out of here guys! Love you!" I shout to my family. I roll my eyes as Matt comes scrambling down the stairs. I'm surprised he isn't drooling at Alexa already. I mean he is so desperate for her he might as well jump on her and starting kissing her.

"Alexa's here?! Why?" Matt gasped.

"Because we're going to dinner. You know, some of us actually have a life." I retort as I shut the door. I tell Alexa he's on our tail so she slams on the gas. I guess she doesn't want any of his 'baby come back to me' crap.

When we are a good distance away, Alexa breaks the silence, "Carolyn!"

"Hi."

"It's great to see you! We haven't talked in forever!"

"I know! You look amazing!" I say back, looking at her black and white tribal print Givenchy skirt and Kitson leather studded cuffs.

"I have a surprise for you," Alexa giggles, "but you're going to have to wait until after dinner."

I smile. I love surprises! Alexa never disappoints....omigosh! Lilly! I need to make sure we're still on for tomorrow! I completely forgot. I thrust my hand into my dainty Coach bag and search around for my beloved Swarovski Crystal bedazzled BlackBerry.

MY MOBILE: we still on 4 tomorrow?

LILLY'S MOBILE: yep

LILLY'S MOBILE: I'm really excited 2 go shopping

MY MOBILE: ☺!!!!

Omigosh! She has no idea we're going to Hawaii!

LILLY'S MOBILE: ☺ ☺ ☺

MY MOBILE: gtg... with Alexa ttyl

LILLY'S MOBILE: bye

I feel Alexa's eyes on me and I blush. Texting in front of a friend you haven't seen for a month probably isn't the most polite thing to do...especially if she's a celebrity who is used to ALL of the attention. Oops.

"Who was that?" Alexa asks using her acting skills to cover up the fact that she's probably thinking, "Why the hell did you just totally zone me out!?"

"Sorry…" I try to think of something better to say then, 'oh, I was just making sure my friend could still go to Hawaii with me tomorrow.' So I quickly lie, "Matt wanted to know if you missed him."

Alexa is silent and I search for words to fill the silence.

"I hope there are no paparazzi."

"You hope? I don't get why. I mean I'm the one whose life they make miserable! You? You're the one who gets at least seven covers on hot gossip magazines for being seen with me. If I was on the cover it would be some ridiculous headline like: "Alexa Kipley is pregnant!" or "Is America's favorite teen actress losing it?" Alexa laughs, a little on the hysterical side if you ask me. Maybe she is losing it.

I giggle. I can never tell if Alexa actually likes being a celebrity. One minute, she is going on about how awesome the "beautiful life" is and another she is like a whiny two year old who complains about everything! Alexa is probably my hardest friend to read.

Alexa takes her keys out of the car and tucks them into her Chanel bag. She swings herself out of the car as I clumsily stumble out. Yeah, that just shows how much grace I have. I know, you're jealous.

Alexa flips her golden blonde hair as she tells me to catch up. We sit at a table outside and the moist California air settles on our shoulders. The waitress lights the candle at our table and I take a deep breath breathing in the sweet aroma of pomegranate citrus.

♥♥♥

I swear Pepperoni & Co. serves the best bread in the world. It's like a trip to Cloud 9; warm cheesy pizza tucked into crunchy garlic bread...omigosh it's amazing. Pepperoni & Co. also makes the best soda in the entire world. Yeah, they make soda. It's called Poppy Soda Pop; imagine your favorite two sodas combined and that's Poppy Soda Pop. I mean that figuratively, of course.

When we're in Alexa's car, after eating a delicious dinner, she puts a blindfold on my eyes. "No peeking. I don't want you to ruin your own surprise."

I listen to the engine hum as we zoom across...whatever road we're on...and it's boring.

"How long am I going to be sitting like this?"

Alexa laughs, "Not too long. Oh, I don't know, five more minutes."

"Okay," I huff. One thing you should know about me is I am not, in the least bit, patient. Five minutes might not seem long to you, but it is an eternity to me if that five minutes is to be spent waiting for a surprise.

For once in my life five minutes goes quickly. I feel the car jerking to a stop below me. I hear Alexa unbuckling her seat belt and slamming the door as she gets out of the car. I wait (and, yes, there's a first time for everything) patiently. Alexa slips the blindfold off my eyes after she helps me out the car. I look around and my eyes feast upon gorgeous men, dazzling women, and adorable kids. All I can see are flashbulbs going off everywhere and a giant poster smack in front of my face: *The High School Sweatheart* starring Alexa Kipley and Harris O'Smith. Harris stars on the romantic comedy *Hitting the Target* which is produced by the same network as *Ignorance is Bliss*.

"OMIGOSH!" I scream, "YOU DIDN'T TELL ME YOU WERE IN A MOVIE! HOW DID I MISS THE HEADLINES, THE PREVIEWS, HOW DID I MISS THIS?! CONGRATULATIONS! THIS IS FANTASTIC!"

No, really, I have no freaking idea how I missed this. I can be so completely clueless.

Alexa laughs, "Well, you must be pretty naïve to have missed everything. But, you probably didn't notice in the previews because in the movie I'm wearing a brunette wig and green contact lenses. And, as a matter a fact, for some reason there weren't many commercials...so yeah. Now come on! I brought some dresses for us to change into. I don't want to go to my first movie premiere in some Lucky Jeans and an Old Navy tee."

Alexa and I duck into a nearby bathroom and slip into the gowns she brought. They are unbelievable. Somehow she was able to get her hands on two Valentinos. Mine is a sheer knee length dress almost completely covered in tan flowers. Alexa looks absolutely stunning in a bold red sleeveless gown with a full (total Cinderella worthy) skirt paired with Gucci stilettos.

I have to tell Matt! He will be so unbelievably jealous! Matt has yet to do a movie or be considered for a part. However, the beloved press doesn't know that. Magazines like *People* and *OK!* are under the impression that, 'Matt Martin is simply taking his time on picking his next project. He says, "I just want my next big thing to, you know, actually be a BIG thing. Don't worry though I'm not losing touch with top directors, I'm just waiting for the right one, you know, I want us to click."'

Isn't that stupid? I mean, personally, when Matt says this he is coming off as some overly picky actor who thinks he's too good for all the directors out there.

Alexa and I gingerly step on to the red carpet and I'm blinded almost immediately by the camera flashes. My ears are ringing like an alarm as hundreds of reporters, at least one from every magazine, newspaper, and gossip channel in the world, shout out questions to us...well actually not *us* more like *Alexa,* but still I have to hear them.

People magazine: "Alexa! Tell me what it's like to star in a movie directed by Owen Bill! Is your hottie costar Matt Martin on *Ignorance is Bliss* a good kisser?"

Alexa posed for the photographer accompanying the reporter, "It's amazing. Owen Bill is such a wonderful guy and a pleasure to work with. I actually look forward to a day of work rather than groan when my alarm goes off." She giggled, "Matt, oh I just love him to death! He has a fun personality and, of course, he is gorgeous! And his kissing..." Alexa winked, walking off leaving the reporter wanting more. Say hello to the cover of *People.*

Glamour magazine: "What is *your* favorite movie, Alexa?"

"This one, of course!" Alexa gasped as if she was shocked someone would ask such a question.

OK! magazine: "Are you excited for your mom's new clothing line?"

"Yes, my mom is truly an amazing woman and only hope I can grow up to be as awesome as her. Her line fits so many different personalities and suits all ages. Check it out at www.kipleydesigns.com!"

I stifled a chuckle. If I knew Mrs. Kipley, she had poor Alexa up all night rehearsing those very lines.

US magazine: "How did you and Matt Martin call it quits? How did you feel? Is it true he cheated on you?"

I watched Alexa grimace at the question, but she brushed it aside and plastered on her best toothy Hollywood grin, "We were just two different people who were too quick to get serious. All is well between us and I do not yet know the truth of the cheating rumor."

Wow. Talk about being a good liar. If I was Alexa I would have ratted out Matt for all its worth, but I guess if you have a career and you don't want to be overloaded with bad publicity that isn't what you want to do. However, that is what you want to do if that guy is your big bro...not that I would ever date my brother or anything.

Another reporter from E! channel caught on and asked, "Did you ever consider cheating on him?"

I gasped at that question. What was *that* supposed to mean? Do they really think Alexa would do that?! I normally wouldn't butt in on Alexa's interview, but really? Really, E!, really?

I looked at the reporter who was watching Alexa expectantly. She was pretty, but that could only be expected since everyone in Hollywood seems to be (with a little help of a few plastic surgeons). However, I think her beauty was natural. Lucky. Well, natural asides from her makeup, but who doesn't wear makeup? Her hair was a rich chocolate brown and her fair skin was nicely spotted with freckles. She was thin, but not deathly skinny and she wore a cute Antonio Melani blazer. She was probably the perfect image countless women aspired to look like.

Before Alexa could answer I blurted, "Of course Alexa would NEVER have cheated on Matt! She is way deeper than that, why would you even ask such a completely ridiculous question?"

Oh no. Flashbulbs erupted. Great, now there will be a wonderful picture of me losing my cool, which is totally and completely not flattering.

The beautiful E! reporter turned to me aghast, "And, who might you be?"

I nervously swallowed; this was not part of my plan. "Carolyn Martin. I'm, um, Matt Martin's little sister."

"Oh," she smiled sweetly, "And why are you here, hon?"

"She's my guest." Alexa interrupted, "We've been best friends as long as I've been on *Ignorance is Bliss.*"

Aw! Alexa says I'm her best friend? Yay! I mean she probably is saying it mainly to butter up the agitated E! reporter but, whatever.

The beautiful reporter smiles the same sweet smile, "How sweet."

"Now, um, if you'll excuse us we better make our way to the auditorium." Alexa smiles, poses for the cameras, then we take a group shot and scurry to the next reporter begging for answers.

As we make our way Alexa scolds me. Sigh. "What was that?! I cannot believe you did that! I mean it wasn't horrible or anything, but still. Why?"

"I just couldn't believe they would even think that about you. Cheating on Matt, I mean," I mutter. This is so embarrassing! I'm being scolded by someone who's only a year older than me!

"Well, don't ever do that again. Ever. It isn't like I don't appreciate you standing up for me, but that was not the time or place," Alexa tells me curtly. Omigosh I could not be anymore humiliated than I am right now. Pooh.

"I'm really sorry."

Alexa hugs me and coos, "Don't worry about it. It's okay."

Phew! At least that turned out okay! We walk on and Alexa begins to ignore even more reporters until one catches our interest and, even more interesting, he is talking to me.

"Carolyn Martin! Oh! CAROLYN MARTIN! OVER HERE! NO, OVER HERE!"

I glance over at the reporter nervously and eye him up and down. He was tall, early twenties, and if I do say so myself incredibly cute, but why does he want to talk to me? I look back at Alexa and she pushes me over.

"Yes?" I ask timidly.

"Hello," the reporter holds out his hand and I hesitantly shake it, "I'm Wilson Walker from *Gilbertson Gossip* and I had a few questions for you."

"Okay…" I hesitate, what if I say something I'm not supposed to?

"Do you watch the hit TV show *Ignorance is Bliss* in which your brother, Matt, and friend, Alexa, star on?"

I smile, "Yes, why wouldn't I? It's the best show ever!"

"Who's your favorite character on the show beside Daniel or Harper?"

I pause. I totally would have said Alexa's character Harper and probably Matt's Daniel, I guess, to look good. "I really have fun watching Daisy Cladsten's character Katie! I think she plays a great rival to Harper and is quite excellent at portraying the backstabbing cousin who can still be nice at times."

"Thank you." Wilson scribbles down some notes. "Is Matt as much a wooing, kind-hearted, romantic in real life as he is on screen?"

I want to scream to Wilson Walker NO! That's what I hate about Daniel's flawlessly charming personality, everyone assumes that Matt is the absolute same way! Only two things are the same between Daniel and Matt. They are both athletic; even though Daniel more than Matt. And, they are both charismatic; except Daniel is sensitively endearing and Matt is a cheating player. Well, maybe not quite a player, but same difference.

"Yes! Matt is a great brother and any girl would be lucky to have him," I lie.

Actually half of what I said is true. I mean Matt is a nice brother and girls do love him. And, any girl would be lucky to have him...to herself.

♥♥♥

About 40 reporters and 400 questions answered later, Alexa and I walk into the theater. I'm very excited, not only because Alexa is the star of the movie, but I love the storyline. *The High School Sweatheart* is about two high school students, Leslie (Alexa Kipley) and George (Harris O'Smith) who miss their flight home during their school trip in New York City, New York. The two are forced to fend for themselves in the city that never sleeps. Their cause is not helped by the fact that Leslie is still pissed at George for cheating on her while they were dating a few months back. Therefore, we can only wonder if they'll fall in love or split farther apart.

We walk out of the theater about 30 gasps (1 onscreen and 29 off), 24 sobs (11 onscreen and 13 girly off), 45 passionate kisses/make-outs (7 onscreen and 38 off between various couples), and 240 content faces (scattered onscreen and off throughout the movie) later. It's safe to say, that people loved *The High School Sweatheart*, especially since it ended with Leslie and George getting back together. Awwwwww.

The movie reminded me too much of Alexa and Matt's cheating mishap...

3. I Get Around

I just remembered something that is probably majorly important for tomorrow...Lilly might need to know to pack for a weekend in Hawaii. I call her right away. I can't wait to tell her the news!

"Hello?" I called her home and, as usual, her brother Jeff answers.

"Hey Jeff..." I start.

"LILLY!" I hear him yell on the other end.

"Hey, Carrie! What's up? I'm so excited to go shopping tomorrow!" Lilly peeps.

"Hi. Yeah about shopping tomorrow I have some news for you."

"Ugh Carolyn, you aren't canceling on me are you?!" Lilly sounds annoyed.

"No! Let me finish! WE ARE GOING TO THE CALVIN KLEIN FASHION SHOW IN MAUI INSTEAD!" I scream.

"NO WAY! AHHH! I CAN'T WAIT! IT WILL BE SO FUN! OMIGOSH CARRIE! I AM SO EXCITED!" Lilly screams.

"Yep," I am so good! "Your parents know and it's fine with them. We'll leave tomorrow at around 11:00 a.m. and be in Hawaii 'til Tuesday evening! Like an extended weekend in heaven! Now get your butt to your room and pack!"

Lilly giggles, "Okay! Love you Carrie!"

"I love you too! Bye!" I hang up convinced I'm the best friend to walk the planet.

♥♥♥

LILLY'S MOBILE: yay! we r going 2 Hawaii!

MY MOBILE: ☺ r u already 2 go? we'll be ovr in a hour

LILLY'S MOBILE: oh yeah!!

MY MOBILE: nice. ttys

LILLY'S MOBILE: l8r Carolyn

"CAROLYN?! ARE YOU UP?!" my mom shouts.

"YES! I'VE BEEN UP SINCE LIKE 7 MOM!"

"DON'T SNAP AT ME CAROLYN!"

"I'm not."

"WHAT? I COULDN'T HEAR YOU!"

"I SAID I'M NOT!"

"DON'T RAISE YOUR VOICE AT ME!"

"OTHERWISE YOU CAN'T HEAR ME!"

"YOU'RE SNAPPING HONEY!"

Omigosh, forget it. I swear sometimes my mom doesn't hear herself talk! No worries though, my handy dandy BlackBerry can solve this.

MY MOBILE: Mom, I wasn't snapping at you. You just couldn't hear me if I didn't shout...I tried.

It really gets on my nerves sometimes how my parents make me text them in proper grammar.

MOM'S MOBILE: I'm sorry honey. I know that now, you know how I feel about respect.

MY MOBILE: I love you! Now I have to pack ☺

MOM'S MOBILE: Make sure to pack something attractive! Maybe some makeup too...how do you feel about dying your hair? We could get it done in Hawaii! Maybe Lilly's, too. She could use some low lights.

I don't know why I even try with my mom sometimes.

♥♥♥

Matt, his personal security guard Neil, my mom, and I pull up to Lilly's house at 11:00 a.m. I am beyond thrilled to spend a weekend in Hawaii with my best friend! It'll be a blast!

I skip up to the Thomas' house in my favorite traveling outfit. I'm wearing straight leg True Religion jeans, a white tank from J.Crew with little flowers, some cute flats from American Eagle Outfitters, and I have my trusty camel leather Dooney & Bourke handbag. I knock on the front door, Lilly opens it and screams, hugging me, and jumping up and down. We scream for awhile until, of course, my brother, Matt the diva, shouts for us to hurry up or he'll be late for Miley Cyrus' party.

We run in Lilly's house and we get her things while singing "I Get Around" by the Beach Boys. We've sang it together when we're really happy since 6th grade when we had this whole Beach Boys phase.

At the airport, after we're through security, Lilly and I dart into one of those little magazine/snack shops ready to fill our arms with gossip and beauty magazines and Swedish Fish.

"Omigosh! Carrie! Look at this!" Lilly thrusts a new issue of *Seventeen* in my face.

"Eeeeewwwww," I sputter.

Apparently my brother, Matt Martin, teenage heartthrob, the "sensitive" modern day Romeo of TV, was voted the top of "Seventeen's Hot Guys of Summer." He gets a three page spread of "sexy" pictures of him, cheesy quotes, and a self-serving biography. I flip to one of his "smoldering" pictures and I'm shocked. Matt looks like he's an ad for the Armani cologne *Acqua Di Gio*. He's sitting by the ocean gazing at the camera with water dripping down his perfectly toned chest. This wouldn't do. No, no, no, it just wouldn't work for me.

"Pinch me."

"What? Why?"

"Look at this picture of Matt," I show her the Armani like picture of Matt.

"Whoa," she gasps, "He looks amazing."

"I know! That's the problem!" I bring my voice to a whisper, "He looks...*attractive.*"

"Well, of course he does! How long does it take you to realize everyone *loves your brother.*"

This is too much for me. I can't think my brother actually looks good. Let alone hot. It's just not right! It's like breaking the golden rule of siblinghood! And, my best friend thinks he's hot. Lilly, my partner in "brother-pranking," agrees with *Seventeen* magazine; that he is the "Hottest Guy of Summer." Puh-lease.

Now the decision at hand is...do we show Matt what the world of teenage girls think? Do we blow up his ego even more than it already is? I think not. I'll just hope he never finds out. Matt Martin is too self-obsessed as it is.

I walk over to Lilly and look over her shoulder as she texts.

LILLY'S MOBILE: hey. congrats

MATTY'S MOBILE: what 4?

LILLY'S MOBILE: being the sexiest guy of *Seventeen*...duh

MATTY'S MOBILE: YES!!!!!!!!!!!!!!!!!!!!!!!!!!!!!!!!! IM TOO SEXY TO CONTROL NOW!!

LILLY'S MOBILE: ☺ ttyl ☺

MATTY'S MOBILE: yea leave! i'm too sexy 4 u anyway.

"Why'd you tell him?!" I scold.

"I thought he would want to know," Lilly says simply.

"Then why would you tell him?! We never tell him what he wants!"

"Yeah...about that..." Lilly slurs.

"What?"

"Did I ever mention I think I *like* Matt?"

4. There Are Two Types of Chemistry

What?!

"I'm sorry," I pause, "What'd you say? I think I misheard you."

"I like Matt. Actually I'm a little in love with him," Lilly says dreamily.

"Lilly, *how* do you love him? Do you *even* hear yourself?" I shout.

"Carolyn! Chill. I just have a crush on him! It isn't like we've even gone out...yet."

I sigh. This is a dream, it must be. How can Lilly love my brother? Is that even legal? I'm just kidding...kind of.

"Fine," I sigh, "I support your 'love'."

Lilly squeals, "Yay! I just adore Matty! He is so dreamy! I mean he's cute, funny, romantic, smart..."

I daze off this is so boring. Wait! Did she just say Matt is smart? Puh-lease. He's lucky he passed Kindergarten. Well, at least she hasn't mentioned sensitive.

"...did I mention cute? Oh, and he's fit, probably a good kisser, and he's sensitive!"

I choke on my Diet Pepsi that I just bought. Seriously, I'm concerned, is Lilly insane? Is she the one dreaming here?

"Wait! Sensitive? You've got to be kidding me."

"Well, I'm not. He's totally sensitive! Like Daniel."

Okay, really? Who thinks cheating qualifies as sensitive?

"You know what happened with him and Alexa right?" I wait for her enlightenment, but she just sits there. "He cheated on her Lilly. *Cheated*."

Lilly sighs, "Common, Carrie! That was with Alexa, not me! Besides, so he cheated once? No big deal!"

"Lilly, Matt kissed another girl while Alexa was in the bathroom during one of their dinner dates. I coincidentally was in the restaurant the same night because I was on a date with Harris O'Smith..."

"You dated Harris O'Smith?!" Lilly interrupts.

"I guess you could say that, I mean that was like the only date we ever went on. That's not the point though, the point is..."

"Was he a good kisser?"

"Sure, yeah, I don't care! That isn't what I'm talking about! Anyways, I saw Matt kissing the mystery girl…"

"Carolyn?"

" What?!"

"Was it fun?" She wiggled her eyebrows suggestively. Pervert.

"Omigosh! Will you shut up?! Just listen to me! I saw Matt…"

Lilly looked confused, "So…you're saying it wasn't fun? I find that incredibly hard to believe seeing that he's Harris O'Smith."

"Lilly listen to me! I saw Matt kissing this mystery girl when he was dating *Alexa*. Matt wasn't single, he wasn't just casually dating Alexa, they were *exclusive*."

"Oh…well…that was then, this is now!" she hushed her voice to a whisper, "He wouldn't cheat on *me*. Would he? I mean he just couldn't."

Is Lilly not getting the picture? It's basic math! It's totally clear that what happens once can happen again.

Matt + Alexa = Love

Matt + Other girl = -Alexa

Me + [(Matt + Other girl)/Alexa] + Tell Alexa = Break-up

Lilly's new love = New cheating disaster + Broken heart

But, of course, Lilly was never among the most attentive of us during math class.

5. "O, Romeo, Romeo! Wherefore Art Thou Romeo?"

When we arrive in Maui Lilly's still silent. She refuses to speak to me, no matter how much I try to talk to her, she's like a mime. We walk off the plane silently. And, the silence continues all the way to the resort.

Honestly, I have nothing against Lilly liking my brother. I just want to make sure she knows who she's dealing with. I wouldn't be able to endure Lilly's misery if Matt made the ridiculous mistake to cheat on her. Matt wouldn't be able to either, not after I'm done with him. In fact, he'd never cheat again in his whole life.

MY MOBILE: we need 2 talk

MATTY'S MOBILE: well i'm like right next 2 u...can't we actually talk??

MY MOBILE: no Lilly might hear & shut me up

MATTY'S MOBILE: ok i'm listening

MY MOBILE: how do u feel about Lilly? not as my friend. as a girl

MATTY'S MOBILE: she's a knock out

MY MOBILE: would u evr ask her out?

MATTY'S MOBILE: hmm...

MY MOBILE: r u interested??

MATTY'S MOBILE: i guesso...

MY MOBILE: gr8! now we nvr discussed this ok?

MY MOBILE: now go ask her

MATTY'S MOBILE: yea...i think i will!

Now who's the best friend ever? Me.

I glance over at Matt and he looks at me. I give him thumbs up.

Matt clears his throat, "Lilly?"

I swear Lilly's heart leaps out of her chest, "Yes?"

Matt goes into I'm-so-nervous-will-she-say-yes? mode, "Iwaswonderingifyouwantedtogooutwithmetonight."

"What? I didn't get that." I could tell Lilly was toying with him. Cruel.

"I was wondering if you wanted to go out with me tonight. I mean, you don't have to. I was just curious if you would be interested in maybe seeing a movie and getting something to eat. I'm sure there's a good movie out...like um..." Matt turns a bright red and looks to me for help.

Awww, he's embarrassed! That's so sweet! I try to think of a movie. *The High School Sweetheart* was totally romantic and up Lilly's ally, but would it be a problem it stars Alexa? Matty's ex?

"*The High School Sweetheart* looks good." Lilly blurts, then blushes. Well, apparently Lilly wasn't worried about the movie choice.

"Okay," Matt agrees, "We could see that." He smiles, then Lilly smiles, then I smile.

Aren't I the little matchmaker?

6. French Kisses

"...it was absolutely amazing. We ate at Fleming's and then saw *The High School Sweatheart* and it was wonderful! Then we began to drive home, but Matt suggested we stopped to get ice cream at Ben & Jerry's. So I sat in one chair and he in the other, I ate Cherry Garcia and he had Rocky Road. Then we drove back here in the dark intimate limo and he had his arm around me. It was just perfect!" Lilly gushes for the third billionth time about her date with Matt.

I sighed, "Wow Lilly. You are totally, completely, and utterly smitten...with *my* brother."

Lilly sighed dreamily, "Yeah..."

"Did you kiss?"

"No, I...um...I...don't...believe we did." Lilly's face fell like when milk is tipped out of a glass.

"Oh." I struggled to find the right words, the words that would express to her that that's okay, not ideal, but okay. "That's alright. I mean hardly any couples kiss on their first date, I mean, unless you're like a total slut, but obviously you're not." Boy, I was having a lot of trouble getting these words out, but I knew someone who could help.

MY MOBILE: hey its me & we need help

ZACHARY'S MOBILE: hello chica. what can I do?

MY MOBILE: Lilly met a guy

ZACHARY'S MOBILE: ooh who???

MY MOBILE: actually the guy is um matty

ZACHARY'S MOBILE: matty?! ooh her taste has definitely improved ☺

MY MOBILE: yep well the problem is that they didn't kiss ☹ Lilly wants me to make that happen asap

ZACHARY'S MOBILE: hmm...where r u?

MY MOBILE: the four seasons in maui

ZACHARY'S MOBILE: omg me 2! vogue conference as always...

MY MOBILE: we're in room 233, want to come over?

ZACHARY'S MOBILE: i'll come over right now

Zachary is 17 and he's tall, dark, and handsome. He loves clothes and everything gossip. I was in New York City because Matty was going through this phase when he tried to have a second-job as a singer. Matty can sing, but on his album his voice was so synthesized that live he was a total let down. Anyways, Matty was on his "No Worries" tour and while he was busting his butt singing live under hot sweaty lights, I went shopping; I was in Loehmann's trying to decide if I should buy this super cute sky blue Prada mini dress when Zachary came by and was all, "Omigosh that is *so* your color." Guess who ended up $800 poorer (sorry Daddy!), but one dress richer? Me. So, Zachary and I have been friends ever since.

There was a thump on the door and I scrambled to get it, "Hello," I said cheerily.

"Carolyn, darling, how are you?"

"Fantastic!"

I went to give Zachary a hug, but he shooed me off, "Kiss kiss, but I can't afford to wrinkle this suit. It's from Gucci's new summer line and I was on the waiting list for like *ever*."

"Hey Zack," Lilly sniffed (Oops, I hadn't noticed she was on the verge of tears).

"Zach*ary*," he corrected. "Ooh, my sweet little Lilly of the Valley, what is the matter?"

Lilly let out a sob and wailed out the whole story while Zachary listened intently, "Oh Lilly, it's quite alright. Almost no one is ever kissed on their first date, overall it sounds like you and Matt had a ravishing time. I would not let this get to you."

I stifled a laugh, Lilly? Not letting something get to her? Ha! Good luck with that!

Lilly sniffed and wiped her eyes smearing her mascara, "I...I...I guess you're right."

"Of course I'm right," Zachary cooed while he wiped off the smeared mascara and whipped out a tube of Maybelline Great Lash Waterproof mascara and reapplied it on Lilly, "Now, not to worry, Carolyn and I will fix this right away."

"Wait...*we* will?" I asked incredulously.

"Yes, Carolyn, we will," Zachary looked at me like duh-you-idiot.

I sighed, "Fine. What are we going to do?"

Zachary clapped his hands, "Delightful! It's time to start operation *French Kisses*."

"*French Kisses*? That's the best name you can come up with? I do not like the idea of Lilly and Matty French kissing, it's totally repulsing."

"Whether you like it or not, they'll get there eventually," Zachary pointed out.

"EW!" I shriek as I throw a pillow at Zachary and then another at Lilly since I did not like how welcome she was looking at the idea.

After about an hour of pillow fighting chaos we had laid down the plan. Lilly would go on another date with Matt, then after a delightfully romantic dinner at The Melting Pot (how do I know that's where Matt will take Lilly? I told him it was her favorite restaurant and that she'd be heartbroken if they don't go). Here they will spend hours finger feeding each other many fondue favorites, but the most romantic, in my opinion, chocolate covered strawberries. After that they would get in the limo to make their way home. May I add that is an hour and a half long way home of which they will have to take quiet and out of the way side roads in order to avoid the extremely over-excited teenagers on their way to the Black Eyed Pea's concert. Then, on one of the many quiet side roads the limo will run out of gas...

♥♥♥

"Wait a minute here," Neil threw up his hands, "You want me to make sure Matt's limo only has half a tank of gas?"

"That is exactly what we just said!" Zachary shouted impatiently, "So will you pretty, pretty please help us out here, Nelson?"

"My name's Neil," Neil informed him through gritted teeth; he turned to me, "Carolyn, your parents *pay* me to keep your brother safe. I can't afford to put my job on the line so you can try to get your little friend her first kiss!"

"Second kiss," I added.

"Is there even a difference?" Neil yelled incredulously.

Zachary gasped, "Of course there is! How could you be so insensitive?! A girl's first kiss is the start of her new, romantic life! A second kiss is like a promise that there are more suitors out there and that she should never give up!"

Neil stared at Zachary, blinking.

Zachary huffed, "It's just really important, ok?"

Neil clucked his tongue and I could practically see the wheels turning in his head, "Fine," he gave in, "I'll do it."

"Promise?" I asked him.

"I promise." Neil assured us, but as he began walking away he grumbled under his breath, "I better be a getting bonus."

7. Love is Blind and Calvin Klein

At the Calvin Klein fashion show I'm sitting in my seat trying not to barf. All worked out in operation *French Kisses*; actually, it worked out a little too well considering Matt and Lilly have seriously not come up for air since their first kiss. It's kind of hard to have some heart to heart time with Lilly when Matt has his freaking tongue jammed down her throat. I'm kidding, of course...kind of.

"Guys, I'm sorry to interrupt and all, but seriously! Can't you get a room?" I shriek.

"Mmmm," Matt takes a breath and detaches himself from Lilly's searching lips, "That's actually..." another kiss, "not a..." more kissing, "bad idea."

"Yeah," Lilly breathes, practically drooling all the way down to her purple Michael Antonio faux leather and satin leopard-print stilettos.

Geez, hormonal anyone? I pull out my BlackBerry and start texting Alexa about Matt's new fancy.

MY MOBILE: lucky u, matt's found someone new & not just anyone new...Lilly

ALEXA'S MOBILE: seriously!? gr8! well 4 me anyways...how'd it happen?

MY MOBILE: lonnnng story

ALEXA'S MOBILE: i've got time

God, I hate when people say that.

MY MOBILE: well yeah so i took Lilly with me to Maui to see the Calvin Klein fashion show 2 make up 4 missing this major horse show she invited me 2 c, right?? it was a total surprise...well anyways, we're in the airport & she sees *Seventeen*'s new issue & basically realizes how hot Matty is & decides, "oh i'm gonna like him now". long story short Zachary and i set them up & I wonder if either of them will evr breathe fresh air again...if u know what i mean

ALEXA'S MOBILE: hmm...well i don't know if i should be happy he likes someone else or totally bummed 4 u :p

ALEXA'S MOBILE: probably both

MY MOBILE: ugh

ALEXA'S MOBILE: well i'd love 2 stay and sympathize with you but i have 2 go, i have 2 get ready 4 "The Girls of *Ignorance is Bliss*" photo shoot. love u and hang in there

MY MOBILE: i thought u said u had time...haha jk...love u 2

I huffed and jammed my BlackBerry back into my new classic brown Louis Vuitton clutch. I looked over at Mr. and Mrs. Hormonal and wasn't surprised to see them kissing like there's no tomorrow. I sighed and stared down out at my outfit. Naturally, when you go to a fashion show you should wear clothes from that designer. Therefore, I was all decked out in Calvin Klein; Calving Klein semi-light wash skinny jeans, a ruffled light blue blouse (on which I had put a white ribbon around the upper waist line), and the Calvin Klein suede gray flats. Calvin Klein, Calvin Klein, Calvin Klein…try saying that ten times fast.

I understand why Lilly and Matt have to be all over each other, I really do. I mean they think they're in love. They think this flame will last forever, and I'm no love expert, but at 15 and going into my sophomore year of high school I've only really been in one "real" relationship and this is exactly how it started. We thought we were in love and we spent all hours together, but then *kaboom* it all came crashing down.

His name was Jake and I thought he was amazing and we went out basically all freshman year. He was on the freshman basketball team and their star point guard. Jake was tall and had rich brown eyes and slightly messy brown hair and I swear had the longest eyelashes I've ever seen.

I had a friend named Clare and in 7th grade she had crushed on him, too, and had tried to work up the guts several times to ask him out, but didn't. Anyways, she had a thing for him and I guess one day it just died down, if only temporarily.

One night during late March, Jake and I were at Clare's party and Jake had gone to get him and me a Pepsi, but it was taking forever and I was getting beyond impatient. Then I got up and went to get a drink for myself thinking maybe he was in the bathroom or catching up with his basketball buddies. But then I found Jake and Clare kissing in front of the Pepsi cooler, but wait it gets better. Clare had a beer in her hand and I could tell was drunk. I was pissed like hell, one because Clare was drinking which was something I never imagined any of my friends would do. Two, Jake was being an asshole and kissing her when he was obviously going out with *me*. And it's not even like Clare was in her right mind, no, Jake was kissing a drunk.

After that I never talked to Clare again no matter how many times she apologized because you know what? I didn't care. It's not like Jake and I had only gone out once so therefore no one really knew about *us.* No, we had been going out the whole year. The day after the party Jake called to apologize and had the typical sob story prepared; 'I don't know what I was thinking and you're the only one for me. I'm sorry I've never said this before, but this event has made me realize how much you mean to me, I love you Carolyn. Forgive me?' I was like, 'Oh, yeah, and I'm sure you'd never mind if I got wasted and went around hooking up with your friends. An eye for an eye right?' We haven't talked since.

I would hate for that to happen to Lilly.

♥♥♥

Coming out of my trance, I look up at the runway and see a beautiful brunette with dark chocolate brown eyes and Matt sees her, too. She is more of Matt's type if you ask me. I mean, do not get me wrong, Lilly is stunning with thick near platinum blonde hair and sky blue eyes. Lilly was of average height and she was thin from weekly Pilates, but her beauty was more princess like. Matt preferred more exotic, which is why he fell for Alexa and now was falling for the beautiful brunette. This is why I knew the thing with Lilly wouldn't last long, and no matter how great Lilly is Matt always thinks someone else is better.

Part Two

Natalie

8. The Princess and the Pea

You know the story *The Princess and the Pea*? When a prince searches the whole world for a princess who when she sleeps on hundreds of mattresses, still notices the pea underneath them all? Then, finally, one girl comes along who surprises him and raves about her awful night's sleep and then the two get married and they live happily ever after.

The problem with Matty and his "princesses" is he is that specific about them. If Matt was able to make all his girlfriends sleep on a pea he would. It will be nearly impossible to actually find him a "princess"! To find Matt a girl who he truly loves, to find him a girl who he loves so much that he isn't distracted by other pretty girls he may encounter, and, of course, she must be a girl who actually likes *him* and not just his *money*.

♥♥♥

After the show, Lilly excused herself to the bathroom. Matt ambled over to where all the models are talking no doubt getting ready to flirt. When he reached them he made small talk with a petite brunette, then he was beckoned by an Australian model with sun-kissed skin and blonde hair and they flirt a bit. Next, he was called by a lanky red head who must have been a fan because she shoved a piece of paper in his face for him to sign. Then, Matt saw her...the beautiful brunette.

Oh no. There is no way Matty is going to make it out of her grasp without a second girlfriend or replacing Lilly as one. I dart over there without even knowing what I'm going to do. All I know is here goes nothing.

I pop up behind Matt giving him a peck on the cheek, "Matty," I coo, "I was looking all over for you..." I glance up at the brunette and act surprised, "I'm sorry I can be so rude sometimes! I don't believe we've met before," I held out my hand, "I'm Carolyn, Matt's girlfriend."

I took a side glance at Matt; his jaw was to the floor. I couldn't help but laugh to myself.

"Oh um I...," I could tell the model was caught off-guard, "I'm Natalie."

"Pleasure. So, um, how did you become a Calvin Klein model? You know sometimes Matt tries to encourage me to become a model since he just thinks I'm so enchanting, but I don't know."

Matt looked at me like, you-are-really-enjoying-this-aren't-you?

Natalie smiled sweetly, "You know, you could actually make a great model! Your red hair is just exquisite and you have great deep blue eyes. Yeah, I've always wanted to be a model ever since I was a little girl and it all just seemed to happen from there."

I smiled and Matt cut in, "Well, Natalie it's been great meeting you. Hey, can I have your number?"

Natalie hesitated, "I don't want to be awkward. I mean, you're in a relationship."

"Oh it's fine! *Isn't* it Carolyn?" Matt said.

I huff and realize there is no way I can say no without looking over protective. "Yeah."

Natalie smiles the same sweet smile and writes down her number, "Ok. Well I'll see you around. I'm going to be here until Tuesday, at the Four Seasons."

"Really?" I replied, "Us, too!"

"I'll talk to you later, Natalie" Matt said.

"Yeah," Natalie sighed with longing in her voice.

I flash a wide smile and added perkily, "Talk to you soon."

Matt starts to walk away and I catch up to him, linking my arm in his, "You know," I laughed, "I could really be a wonderful actor! Maybe I could be on your show!"

Matt unhooked his arm and looked at me like I was the biggest idiot to walk the planet, "Ugh, Carolyn! Why did you do that? You know not everything can always be in your control!"

I frown, "Um sorry for ruining your party bro, but you're *dating* Lilly. And, it seemed like you were pretty in to her during the show."

"Do you not get it? I'm a guy. My emotions are like minutes, always changing. You can't expect me to not notice an absolutely gorgeous girl when I see her!"

"Omigosh Matt, how much of a boy can you be? You wouldn't know a great girl if she hit you in the face."

"Come *on,* Carolyn," we sit on a nearby bench, "As my sister, not Alexa's friend, not Lilly's friend, don't you see how much of my type Natalie is? Put aside all of your anger about what I did to Alexa and your worries about Lilly."

I groan, "I know, I know. Actually the minute I saw her, I knew. I knew you would fall for her and I knew that the second Lilly left you would go chat her up. That's why I pulled that girlfriend stunt, and, by the way, you seriously need to moisturize. Your cheeks are like a desert."

Matt reached up to feel his cheek, "What should I do? Honestly, I don't want to hurt Lilly. I don't want to break-up with her, but I don't want to stay with her and then end up not paying attention to her."

"I'd love to answer, but I have no idea. One side of me wants you to break-up with her so you can take a chance on Natalie. Another side says suck it up and stay with Lilly and I hope maybe you'd realize she's enough for you."

Matt looked at me with sad eyes and I think I could feel my heart break for him. No, Lilly's feelings were on the line, this was no time for pity.

♥♥♥

MATTY'S MOBILE: hey it's me matt

NATALIE'S MOBILE: hi, whats up??

MATTY'S MOBILE: just thinking, i have a hard decision to make

NATALIE'S MOBILE: ☹ can i help?

MATTY'S MOBILE: not really

NATALIE'S MOBILE: ok ☹

MATTY'S MOBILE: actually you can…can u talk later tonight?

NATALIE'S MOBILE: yes, why?

MATTY'S MOBILE: meet me at 7 tonight in the front lobby

NATALIE'S MOBILE: ok…

MATTY'S MOBILE: ok ttyl ☺
NATALIE'S MOBILE: bye ☺ ☺ ☺

I was in the front lobby around 6:45 searching for Lilly. Earlier, after the show she had disappeared to go and explore the various pools. Now about three hours later, I still hadn't found her. Matt had disappeared too. The last I saw of him was after our talk as he texted away to someone on his phone. It was probably Lilly, maybe they went out to dinner or something.

I sighed with relief now that I think I know where Lilly and Matt went off to and settled down into a comfortable leather couch near the front entrance. I pulled out my BlackBerry to check the time; it was seven o'clock. I went to stuff it back in my purse and it slipped out of my hand, and it bounced across the floor and it stopped by another couch. I made my way to retrieve my phone, bent over to pick it up and gasped.

Starting to sit down at a table across the room were Matt and Natalie. My eyes shot wide open and I darted across the lobby and settled at a nearby table covering my face with a bulky *InStyle* magazine.

"Hey," Matt greeted Natalie.

"Hi."

"Thanks for, um, coming."

I knew Natalie was smiling now, "Yeah, no problem. What's wrong?"

"About earlier, with Carolyn that is, I have to tell you something."

I frowned; worried Matt was going to do something stupid.

"Mmhmm?" Natalie edged him on.

Matt cleared his throat, "Carolyn, well, she isn't my girlfriend. Carolyn's my little sister, she's 15, and she recently set me up with her best friend, Lilly. Lilly's my girlfriend, and when Carolyn saw me go over to talk to you she got worried I was going to do something to jeopardize my relationship with Lilly. So, she pretended she was my girlfriend, I guess so you wouldn't get any ideas.

"I appreciate what Carolyn did because I would feel horrible if I ruined everything with Lilly. However, the issue is, I can't get you out of my head. You are absolutely gorgeous and sweet and I feel like I can tell you anything. This is obvious since I'm telling you all this now, so it would really help if you would tell me if you feel the same way about me."

Could he be any more quixotic? What is this "I feel Iike I can tell you anything…" crap? They just freaking met!

"Wow. I don't know what to say..." I could hear Matt hold his breath, "Matt, you seem like an amazing guy. The minute I saw you I could feel my heart stop and I know that sounds cheesy, but it's true. You are a pretty hot guy, Matt. You really are. I admire your courage to tell me all this, it's really romantic in a way..." Natalie sighed.

"Would you ever go out with me?"

"Yes." Natalie breathed.

"Cheese balls," I muttered spitefully.

I knew Matt was smiling from ear to ear now as he clapped his hands and said, "Then I am going to go break up with Lilly and then you can count on me to come ask you out!"

My jaw dropped to the floor. This. Is. So. Not. Good.

"Matt..." Natalie sounded nervous now.

I heard Matt get up, "We can talk later. I have to go," then Matt strutted away oblivious to how he was about to break Lilly's heart and how I was about to break his face.

I jumped out of my chair and followed Matt, when I caught up I whacked him on top of the head with all my might.

"Hey! What the hell?" Matt turned around, "Carolyn! What is your freaking deal?"

"What's *my* deal? What's *your* deal?! You're the one about to break Lilly's heart!"

"What?" Matt asked, but then realization washed over his face, "You were listening to me talk to Natalie!"

"Wow, Matt. I couldn't have figured that out if my life depended on it," I said sarcastically.

Matt stuck out his tongue like a six year old, "So what do you recommend I do? You said a side of you thought I should go out with Natalie."

"I didn't think you would actually do it!" I hissed.

Matt hushed his voice to a whisper, "Carolyn, this feels right to me. I feel more comfortable with Natalie than Lilly. Don't get me wrong, Lilly's beautiful and a great kisser, but..."

I sighed, "Matty, I just don't even know what to say. I give up. Do whatever you want." And with that I walked away.

9. Revenge is Naked

It was official. Matt and Natalie were now dating. I knew this the exact minute Matt walked into the hotel room after he talked to Natalie, he just seemed to be floating on air.

Luckily, I had taken the liberty of setting up what seemed like millions of tissue boxes in our hotel room. Then I had immediately called Zachary to fill him in and he insisted on coming down.

Now, Zachary and I were sitting with Lilly surrounded by used tissues. In the background we had Lilly's iPod playing on her "And I Thought He Loved Me" playlist. Matt had just left from telling her it was over and Lilly already was crying her eyes out.

"Why…did…he…have…to…do this…to…me?" Lilly sobbed, "This sucks."

"Oh honey, don't cry," Zachary cooed as he handed Lilly another tissue, "You were too good for that loser anyway!"

I sat silently besides Lilly gently rubbing her back, I felt horrible, all that was good about this situation according to Lilly was at least Matt hadn't cheated on her. Still, it all really sucked.

"Oh Lilly," I whispered, "I'm so sorry."

Lilly wiped her eyes and looked up at me and let out a sigh, "Me, too."

"Now Lilly," Zachary said while walking over to Lilly's iPod, "We do not let mean old boys get us down? Do we?"

Lilly looked up at Zachary like excuse-me-what-do-you-think-Matt-just-did-to-me?

Zachary unplugged Lilly's iPod from its speakers and replaced it with his own. I could see him scrolling through his song list, "Just listen to this powerful woman. Listen to her strength and how she used what her man did to her to make millions of dollars!"

At first I was afraid...

I was petrified...

Then on came Gloria Gaynor singing *I Will Survive*. I giggled and saw Lilly smile.

Slowly I was learning more and more about Natalie. She was 17 and lived in Napa Valley, California. Her parents owned a vineyard and she had a three years old brother. When she wasn't modeling or at school, Natalie loved to go up to Vail, Colorado and ski. Natalie hated to watch TV unless it was the Olympics, but did not mind watching movies. And, her absolute favorite book of all time was *Dear John* by Nicholas Sparks.

Know what is totally weird? All of Matt's girlfriends, who I've actually met, turn out being some of my best friends: Alexa, Lilly (even though we were already friends, whatever), and now Natalie.

You'd think Lilly would despise Natalie, but oddly, Lilly, Natalie, and I have spent every given moment together. It's Monday evening and we're currently enjoying a hot stone massage.

"You want to know something about Matt, Natalie?" Lilly asked.

Natalie turned her head to face Lilly, "What?"

"His favorite flower is cherry blossom."

I let out a loud guffaw and said jokingly, "You can't be serious; I think we all know that his favorite flower is sweet pea. Gosh, get it right, Natalie!"

"How'd you even find that out?" Natalie asked.

"He told me on our first date. I was wearing my new cherry blossom perfume and he noticed it. Then he was like, 'Fun fact about Matt #24, my favorite flower is cherry blossom."

"Weird..." Natalie and I said in unison, and then we erupted in laughter.

"Jinx! One...two...three...four..." Natalie cried.

"Stop!" I screamed. Natalie had a thing for jinxing, and she actually made you buy her whatever number of sodas you stopped her on.

Natalie grinned, "Four sodas, I'd like two Dr. Pepper's, one 7-Up, and one Diet Coke. You can give them to me tonight when we have our sleepover."

"Fine," I grunted.

"So…" Lilly said mischievously, "Have you and Matt kissed yet?"

"No, of course not, we've only been on two dates!"

"So? Matt and I kissed on our second date."

"With the help of a lack of gas and a Black Eyed Peas concert," I added.

"Wait! What about a Black Eyed Peas concert?" Natalie looked at me and asked.

I smiled, "What? I don't know what you are talking about." Lilly laughed.

Natalie rolled her eyes, "Whatever."

"Ladies, your massages are over. Take your time getting up," one of the masseuses said gently.

"Ok, thanks." Lilly smiled.

"Omigosh, that was amazing," Natalie sighed.

"Yeah, it was," I agreed.

"Race you guys to our bathrobes!" Lilly said excitedly.

"Ok." Natalie agreed.

"On the count of three: one…two……three!" I screamed.

I got up from my massage table and scurried across the room to where my fluffy pink bathrobe was hanging. My naked body was shocked by the cold air that was engulfing my slim limbs. I was now seriously missing being rubbed by hot rocks and covered with sheets.

"I win!" I shouted.

I looked back to see where Lilly and Natalie were to see they were still snug and warm in their blanket and going hysterical from just seeing me dart across the room naked.

I put my hands on my hips, "What?" I snapped, "You've never seen someone streak before?"

They were still laughing.

"Well, you know what? Streaking takes skill. You guys are just embarrassed to streak in front of an extreme streaking master like myself," I fumed. If I was a cartoon, smoke would be coming from my ears right now.

They were still laughing, but whatever because they wouldn't be for long.

I stomped over to Lilly's and Natalie's tables and their eyes were still closed and you could see their bodies shaking with laughter through the sheets. Luckily for me, this shaking would ensure that they wouldn't know what hit them...or at least until they opened their eyes.

I dragged over a bunch of pillows and lined them around their beds because even though I temporarily hated them, I didn't want them to get hurt. Then, with speed like a fox, I pushed them both simultaneously out of their beds.

Lilly and Natalie fell with a thump, "OOF," they both moaned.

I was dying of laughter now, almost so I couldn't breathe. Then I looked at them frankly and said, "That's what you get," and stomped out of the room and slammed the door.

Part Three

Grace

10. Drama Princess

Natalie, apparently, has an issue. If you want to go into details, it's an issue with being pushed out of massage beds. Natalie, also apparently, bruises very easily so now her perfect model body was covered in not so perfect little bruises. Furthermore, the second we landed in LAX, I received a call from Natalie's agent reporting the "horrific damage" (a.k.a. little bruises) I had inflicted on her perfect, size zero body. Now, not only does Natalie hate me, but Matt hates me. You cannot imagine the boring lecture he gave me the night when we returned home about how I "wasn't to take my jealousy out on other people even if her life was awesome and mine wasn't." Like I'm even concerned about his relationship with her! I mean, I love Matt, but still, I couldn't care less.

"CAROLYN!" Matt screamed.

"What?" I moaned, leaning over the balcony of my room, to look down at him lounging by our serene, tree-shaded pool, or "private ocean" as he like to call it.

Matt flipped up his aviator glasses and glared up at me, "Just come here, Carolyn. I'm already ticked off at you enough."

A light bulb went off over my head and my throat went dry. Before I even knew it, I knew it: Natalie had broken up with Matt...because of me pushing her out of a freaking massage bed. Damn it, I even put pillows around it! Sissy!

I tiptoed down the stairs if only to increase the mood. Then, I walked up to the doorway leading outside and rested my hip on the door frame.

"Yes?" I whispered. I know, I was being melodramatic, but, hey, I lived with an actor. Doesn't that entitle me to being a little theatrical?

Matt slowly sat up and looked at me; I could see the hurt in his eyes when he looked at me, "Carolyn, why did you push her out of the massage bed?"

Part of me wanted to point out that it was simply revenge for Natalie and Lilly making me streak to my bathrobe. However, I could tell Matt wasn't in the mood for bickering. So instead, I remained silent and let him go on.

"Gosh, Carolyn. I really thought this could work out, Natalie and me. I know you didn't mean to break us up, I do, but still. Damn it, Carolyn! I really liked her! I was serious about a relationship for once in my life. Do you realize how serious that is for me? I could be classified as a "player" to some people, Carolyn. I'm not someone who just walks around falling in love. No, I'm the type of guy who walks around finding the next girl I might want to make-out with.

"Yeah, I was serious about Alexa, but my seriousness for her just kind of scared me into cheating...I was so hopeful that this, this relationship with Natalie would work out."

"I'm sorry, Matt." I breathed.

Matt went on, "And we only were able to go out for two weeks."

"Matt, I'm really sorry! I am."

"Whatever, thanks."

My face fell, I felt horrible, Matty's right. It isn't every day he finds a girl he's serious about. It isn't every day he finds a princess.

♥♥♥

I was lying on my bed fingering my beloved BlackBerry when I came up with *Operation Finding My Brother's Princess*. My new goal for the year was to get Matty a beautiful, funny, caring girlfriend. Seeing that it was summer, this should be a breeze, thousands of pretty teenage girl beach-goers come to California over the summer to soak up some sun. And, hopefully, my brother's future girlfriend will be one of them.

First, I'm going to write down the possibilities to be Matt's girlfriend. I'll start with the girls that already live here and why I think they could be "The One."

Lilly:

- has already dated Matt...evident they have good chemistry
- PRETTY
- fun to be around
- intelligent
- loves Matt's guts ☺
- Reasons why she shouldn't be Matt's "princess": can be clingy, hard to please at times, a little over 3 year age difference, their relationship already failed once, and not to mention it is ILLEGAL for Matt to be dating a minor

Alexa:

- "good kisser"
- PRETTY!!

- *Matt still likes her*
- *successful; smart*
- *Reasons why she shouldn't be Matt's "princess": she's still is furious with Matt, is it a problem they work together?, their relationship already failed once* ☹

I put down my pen and let my mind wander. Would Matt ever settle down? Would he be one of those guys who is still a player when he's 40? 50? 60? Was he a future Hugh Hefner? Ha! I could see him now, lounging around our house in a red silk bathrobe with some pretty platinum blondes trailing behind him decked in lingerie.

I felt sorry for Matt, not having a girlfriend. It really must suck, being a teenage heartthrob who thousands of girls adore, but not being able to actually have a steady relationship! Before Clare ended up ruining Jake and my relationship and I was stuck single again it was nice knowing that you had someone in love with you. Or at least knowing that you had someone who cared enough about you that they would want to kiss you in rain and tell you you're beautiful. Like a Taylor Swift song.

I mean, we certainly weren't the "it" couple at our school. That, by far, would have been Cyndi and Isaac, whose relationship probably could not have been more clichéd. Isaac was a senior, incredibly handsome, and the star quarterback on the football team while Cyndi was a junior and the bubbly, brunette captain of the cheerleading squad.

I was still contemplating this when my BlackBerry buzzed and glanced at the screen.

ZACHARY'S MOBILE: how is the matchmaking going??

MY MOBILE: natalie & matt broke up...and it's my fault ☹

ZACHARY'S MOBILE: oh carolyn, everything happens 4 a reason

MY MOBILE: yeah, but the reason isn't always good

11. Amazing Grace

Love, I have found out, comes in the oddest shapes and forms. It also appears in the weirdest places whether it be a Calvin Klein fashion show or a coffee shop in Beverly Hills.

Matty had gone out for a decaf pumpkin spice latte the Thursday morning after our Natalie break-up talk. As he told me, he had been sitting in a comfy green chair sipping his latte when a beautiful girl walked in. She had straight honey blonde hair and soft brown eyes; her name was Grace. She went up to the counter and ordered, coincidentally, a pumpkin spice latte. As she waited for her drink she "gently tapped her fingers on the counter" and Matty had been "struck by her laid back prettiness."

When she couldn't find a chair, Matt had gotten up to offer her his. They ended up engaging in casual conversation and when Grace turned to go Matt asked Grace whether he'd see her around. She said yes.

Now I was sitting on Matt's king sized bed while he scurried around his closet looking for the perfect outfit for his lunch with Grace today. Yes, you might think this is something *only* girls do, but it isn't. I had been judging outfits Matt suggested for almost half an hour and, frankly, I was bored.

"Matt, if I may be truthful with you, I'm getting tired of searching through your closet. Face it, everything you have is too "Matt the heartthrob celebrity" not "Matt the normal California cutie." You want Grace to see you as just another boyfriend, but better, and love you for who you are and not your designer clothes. I mean, don't you seriously have any clothes from stores found in a mall? Like Aeropostale? Or Macy's?"

"No, I don't, but why does this even matter? Shouldn't I *be myself* and *be comfortable in my own skin*? I mean, she already fell for me at the coffee shop and I was wearing my designer clothes then, so why does it matter now?"

I sighed, he had a point, I hated when he had a point, "It doesn't...but don't you think you should have at least one outfit that cost less than 300 dollars?"

Matt looked at me like I was crazy, "Not really."

If he was stubborn about his designer clothes, I wonder how he'll take the suggestion that he gets serious about one girl...at a time.

12. Assumptions

The minute Matt left for his lunch I went to my room to add Grace to "The One" list. In a sense, Matt was a like a teenage girl who was boy crazy. The girl would have crushes on guy after guy and each crush would become bigger than before. This would continue for a long, long time until she *finally* found her prince charming (a.k.a. her first serious boyfriend).

I took out the list from the top drawer of my dresser, a place I knew Matt would never want to look, and read it over before adding Grace.

Lilly:

- has already dated Matt...evident they have good chemistry

- PRETTY

- fun to be around

- intelligent

- loves Matt's guts ☺

- Reasons why she shouldn't be Matt's "princess": can be clingy, hard to please at times, a little over 3

year age difference, their relationship already
failed once, and not to mention it is ILLEGAL for
Matt to be dating a minor

Alexa:

- "good kisser"
- PRETTY!!
- Matt still likes her
- successful; smart

Reasons why she shouldn't be Matt's "princess": she's still is furious
with Matt, is it a problem they work together?, their relationship
already failed once ☹

Grace:

- has a laid back vibe that Matt finds sexy
- as if by fate, she too ordered a pumpkin spice latte
  this morning
-

My pen hovered above the bullet point I had just
made and I realized I knew little to nothing about Grace.
Was Matt rubbing off on me? I hadn't even seen Grace
and I was already concluding that she may be "The One"
for Matt! What was that phrase about assuming?

Assuming makes an ass out of you and me. If Matt was a sentence... that would be him; he assumes and he's an ass who makes me look like an ass in the process.

13. I Spy with My Chanel Eyes

If someone walked passed me while I sat here behind a rose bush outside the balcony at Pepperoni & Co. wearing my big Chanel sunglasses they would probably call the police to report suspicious behavior. Allow me some time to explain myself. After I realized I knew nothing about Grace and that Matt probably wouldn't date her long enough for her to meet me, I decided to go see her for myself. So now on a bright Thursday afternoon when I could be at the beach with Lilly, I was spying on Matt and Grace.

I knew it was only a first date, so I wasn't expecting any fireworks, but as far as first dates went their chemistry was off the charts. So, sure, it wasn't fireworks *yet*, but there were definitely some sparks. A sure sign that an explosion would be coming soon.

I do realize I'm assuming again, but when you hang out with someone like Matt 24/7 it's hard not to. And is it that bad that I want something amazingly long lasting for my brother? Is it bad that I'm assuming that with Grace he may have an implausibly amorous relationship in store? Sometimes assuming can be just dreaming with exceptionally high hopes and if I said I was simply "dreaming with exceptionally high hopes" it would seem like a good thing. Whereas if I said I was "assuming" it seems like a bad thing.

Matt was now leaning over the table whispering something in Grace's ear. I could see her laugh and a fiery pink blush rush to her cheeks. Matt continued to whisper and Grace's blush turned more crimson. I wondered what he was saying...was he saying something typical-player like, such as, "I already can feel a deep connection between us,"? Or, something earnest and sweet?

As the waiter handed them their drinks, a cola for Matt and iced-tea for Grace, Matt began telling a story to Grace. She nodded, and laughed, and towards the end she reached across the table to squeeze his hand and smile. She had a beautiful smile, not the typical Hollywood bleached white smile, but a nice, straight, slightly ivory smile. When the sun hit her hair you could see a subtle hue of red and her skin would give off a healthy glow.

Matt soon followed his previous story with another, and another, and the whole time Grace never let go of his hand.

♥♥♥

As Grace and Matt left the restaurant my butt was sore and my neck ached. It had been almost two and a half hours since Matt and Grace arrived at the restaurant. And while they were out there flirting, I was here bruising my butt off on the hard brick floor. Ouch.

The date had, by far, been a success. And, yes, I know I said that Lilly and Matt's date was a success, and that I thought Matt and Natalie's relationship might be for real; but, it was nothing compared to what Grace and Matt had going on today. I hope.

As I walked home, I decided to take a detour to Lilly's house to catch up. When I was about three or four blocks away I received a text from Alexa.

ALEXA'S MOBILE: hey...how was the dork's date?

MY MOBILE: haha very funny...i don't know yet, Matt isn't home

Okay, so maybe that was a lie. But I'm not about to tell Alexa that I just spent the last two and a half hours on my ass spying on them.

ALEXA'S MOBILE: oh

MY MOBILE: is something wrong???

ALEXA'S MOBILE: no, not really, just a bit under the weather that's all

MY MOBILE: right...

ALEXA'S MOBILE: seriously.

MY MOBILE: Alexa, don't lie 2 me

My phone rang and I picked it up, "Hello?"

"I'm not lying."

I recognized Alexa's voice immediately and replied, "Alexa, I know you too well. Something's up."

"I'm feeling just a little sick."

"You mean jealous?"

"What? No, I said sick. Do you, like, have a bad connection or something?"

"You're jealous of Matt. Aren't you?" I said in a sing-song voice.

Alexa huffed, "I am *not* jealous."

"Right," I replied in a dead voice.

"Right, I am absolutely 100 percent not jealous of Grace."

"Oh, really, then how did you know her name?"

"What?"

"Her name, Alexa, how did you know her name?" I interrogated.

Alexa hesitated, "Whose name?"

"Grace's name silly, don't play around with me. How did you know her name? And don't say I told you because I never did. All I said was that Matt was going out to lunch with some girl he met at the coffee shop this morning."

"Are you sure? Because I'm almost positive you said something about a girl named Grace." Alexa stuttered nervously. I knew I was close to cornering her.

"No," I smirked, "I'm pretty sure I didn't."

"But…" Alexa struggled.

"But, nothing, Alexa, it's ok that you've been checking up on Matt. We all get a little jealous once in awhile, it's human nature." I sighed, "Just make sure not to cause any trouble."

"Oh no," Alexa assured me, "I would never! I know what it's like to be hurt in a relationship and I would never, *never* want to be the cause of the hurt."

"Ok, well I have to get going. Call you later?" I asked.

"Sure, and Carolyn thanks for being so understanding."

I smiled to the phone, "Yeah, sure, bye."

"Bye." Alexa hung up the phone.

Interesting that Alexa of all people was jealous of Grace. They weren't even in a serious relationship. I could see Lilly being jealous, but Alexa? I would have never guessed.

I was still pondering this in front of Lilly's house when Jeff came out, "*Hey* Carolyn," Jeff slurred his words. He had obviously been drinking with his buddies again. Jeff was 23 and had graduated from USC a couple years back. And to top it off, Jeff wasn't one to say no to a bottle of beer. Jeff wasn't a heavy drinker or anything; he just had a big liking for beer. Emphasis on BIG.

"Jeff," I replied coldly.

"Care, don't go all icy on me," Jeff slurred putting his arm over my shoulder. His breath reeked of beer; he must have drunk more than his usual two bottles of beer this time. Ok, forget what I said earlier, this guy needed to hightail it on out of here and into an AA meeting.

I took Jeff's arm off my shoulders and took a step away from him, disgusted, "Jeff, I'm so not interested."

"Hey," Jeff said putting his hands up, "I never implied anything, but if you had any ideas that's fine with me."

My nose wrinkled up in disdain, "Gross, you are such a pervert."

"And proud of it, baby," Jeff grinned devilishly.

Without another word I ran into the house and dashed up the stairs to Lilly's room. I found her sitting leisurely on her giant, soft green bed reading a book. When she heard my heavy breathing she glanced up, "Hey, I take it you've encountered Jeff already."

"Yeah, he was drunkenly flirting with me. It was so disgusting. How many did he have today?" I asked, plopping down besides Lilly on her bed.

Lilly put her head back, "I don't know, about 3 or 4? Whatever it was, it was too much. His friend Andrew thought it would be smart to bring over two six packs for the two of them." Lilly laughed.

I rolled my eyes, "At least it was legal," I shrugged, "Unlike all those dumb high school guys."

Lilly closed her eyes, "I guess..."

"Ok so moving on, did I tell you Natalie dumped Matt because I gave her bruises?"

"Really? Wow. That is so stupid to give up a guy like Matt because his sister pushed you out of a massage bed." Lilly paused, "Even though I must say, you gave me a hell of some bruises myself."

I smiled apologetically, "Sorry. Well, anyway, now Matt met someone new, her name's Grace....Jones, I think."

Lilly thought it over, "Another girlfriend? Man, Matt sure is girl crazy. Her name's Grace Jones? A little on the plain side, but whatever..."

"You're not jealous are you? I already think Alexa is and I don't need another girl on Grace's tail."

"Alexa's jealous?! The girl he cheated on? Weird."

"I agree, but what about you?"

"Not really, I mean, I'm not saying I'm not upset he dumped me for a girl he wasn't even going to end up staying with, but no. I'm not jealous."

Lilly and I sat in silence for a few moments and then Lilly checked the time on her phone, "Hey, I'd love to stay and chat, but I have to get going. I'm getting some highlights done in like 15 minutes."

"You need highlights? That's ridiculous! Your hair is already like the blondest shade possible." I scoffed.

"I'm not getting my whole head done, silly, just a couple strands here and there. And, my mom," she rolls her eyes like the notion is ridiculous, "is insisting, for a reason God only knows, that I get a trim." she runs a strand of her hair through two short fingernails, "Do I look like I have split ends or something?"

"Ok, I'll see you a bit later, call me tonight." I went and gave Lilly a quick hug, "Now don't come crying to me when your hair is fried with all this treatment you're doing," I joked.

Lilly rolled her eyes and hugged me back, "You worry too much. Did you know that? Besides, it isn't even your hair! Now, do us both a favor and get out of here, Carrie," Lilly joked in return.

I still thought the idea was ridiculous, but I made my way down the stairs while Lilly packed up her purse with almost a million lip glosses.

14. I'm Not Ready

On Matt and Grace's second date Matt decided he would take Grace to the Disney Hall to see "The Lion King," which had apparently been Grace's favorite movie as a little girl. While I helped him decide on his outfit, Matt had let me in on some other things about Grace. With a rare twinkle in his eye that I had never seen before, Matt had told me how Grace is almost 19 years old and going into her sophomore year at Duke University (go Blue Devils!); he explained how she had came to the coffee shop that morning to pick up a pumpkin spice latte for her boss (ok, so maybe her coffee choice wasn't as fated as I thought). Her boss, Grace had told him vaguely, is one of the top movie directors, but would not give Matt the director's name. Matt told me how Grace was the third of five siblings: three brothers and a sister, and that Grace's dad owned a Mercedes Benz car dealership in Beverly Hills and her mom worked as an assistant for Marc Jacobs.

Matty also told me how Grace had explained to him up front right away, that no matter how serious they got she wasn't sure she was ready to really get "physically involved" in a relationship. Even though I agree with Grace's decision, I couldn't help but be alarmed when Matt told me this. I had no idea what Matty felt about this. Granted, he is a virgin (I know! A virgin in Hollywood! Alert the media!), but he also is used to girls falling literally all over him. But, he seemed content and as if he totally agreed so, I guess it was all ok with him I just hoped that his opinion wouldn't change.

15. King of the Jungle

Just like Simba, when Matt returned from his date he had the presence of a king. He was *glowing*. No kidding! He was beaming from ear to ear and his eyes seemed to sparkle. He had a bounce in his stride I hadn't seen since he won his first Emmy for *Ignorance is Bliss*. What did this mean?

"Hey Matty," I smiled at him from my seat on the couch where I had been watching "Glee" as he walked into the living room, "How'd it go?"

"Amazing," Matt plopped down beside me on the couch and went on, "I honestly didn't how fun it could be just being near a girl and not having a make-out session," he joked.

I laughed and rolled my eyes, "Great! So anything of note happen?"

"Eh," Matt shrugged, "Not really...except for, you know, this little something."

I leaned in closer, intrigued, "No, I don't know. Care to enlighten me?"

"We'll see."

"Ugh!" I shrieked, smacking his arm, "You're so mean. You are killing me here!"

A hint of a smile played on Matt's lips, "Nah, really, you wouldn't be that interested."

"Pleeeeeeease? Come on, Matt! Just tell me! Don't make me leak you're potty training photos to the media!"

"Wait, what? You have potty training pictures of me?" Matt asked me incredulously.

I shrugged, "For black mailing purposes."

Matt finally gave in, "I kissed her good night."

"Aww," for some reason my heart melted. "Really? That's so sweet! Give me all the details! When, where, all of it, I need the details!" I squealed.

"Why?" Matt stalled, "Are you thinking of writing a book about it or something?"

"Omigosh, Matt, will you stop stalling and just tell me?"

♥♥♥

Later that night, I sat on my bed reading *Message in a Bottle* when I found myself no longer able to focus on Garrett's heart wrenching letter to Catherine. I put my book down and decided to text Lilly.

MY MOBILE: can't sleep, figured u were still up doing summer reading

LILLY'S MOBILE: maybe...

MY MOBILE: this is why it's smart to finish your reading early...like me :p

LILLY'S MOBILE: overachiever

MY MOBILE: slacker!

LILLY'S MOBILE: whatever. what's up Carrie?

MY MOBILE: couldn't sleep, remember??

LILLY'S MOBILE: nope

MY MOBILE: what about you?

LILLY'S MOBILE: i met a girl today

MY MOBILE: so? what's so important about that?

LILLY'S MOBILE: it was MAGDALENE JULE

MY MOBILE: OMG OMG OMG that is so cool!! what was she like? was she just as pretty in person? did u get an autograph & picture? you better have got me an autograph....OMG ☺

LILLY'S MOBILE: amazing & yes 2 everything else!! but anyways, guess what she told me after i mentioned i knew matt martin?

MY MOBILE: what?

LILLY'S MOBILE: "tell him that i'm starring in the upcoming romantic comedy directed by Cole Collins

& that Cole's interested in having him be the leading man"

MY MOBILE: OH. MY. GOD. THIS IS HUGE!!!! THIS IS LIKE MATT'S FIRST MAJOR MOVIE OFFER!!

LILLY'S MOBILE: I KNOW ☺

MY MOBILE: ok well gotta run!! I have 2 go tell Matty the big news!

LILLY'S MOBILE: Carrie, u do realize its 1 in the morning?

MY MOBILE: it is? oh well!!! I don't care!! TTFN

"MMMMMMMMMMMMMMATT!" I screamed as I dashed into Matt's room, not caring if my parent's heard.

"What?" Matt asked groggily as he sat up in bed wearing his favorite worn sky blue Old Navy tee that really brings out his eyes.

"You'll never guess what Lilly just told me..."

When I had finished explaining Magdalene Jule's movie offer to Matt we dashed down to our parent's room like little kids on Christmas morning. Without hesitation we burst through the double doors and leaped onto their bed causing them to groan like teenagers on a school morning.

"Carolyn? Matt?" my mom peeled off her eye cover that read SLEEPING BEAUTY in curly, pink letters, "What are you two doing?"

My dad was stirred by all the commotion and sat up in bed with his salt-n-pepper hair a mess, "Honey, what's wrong?"

Ignoring my tired parents' comments I squealed excitedly, "MATT WAS OFFERED AN AUDITION FOR COLE COLLINS'S UPCOMING ROMANTIC COMEDY STARRING MAGDALENE JULE!"

"Oh, Matt, that is such exciting news!" my mom gasped, hugging him tightly, "When's the audition?"

"We haven't figured that part out yet," I said sheepishly. Oops. Guess that might have been a good thing to find out...

"No bother," my mom said happily in her high, fairy-like voice, "Oh, Matt, this is fantastic news," she continued to engulf Matt in a giant bear hug.

Mom looked at my dad expectantly, raising her perfectly tweezed eyebrows, "Um, yes, good for you, son!" My dad added awkwardly patting him on the back once he was able to locate it in Mom's arms. "This is a great opportunity."

Little stiff on Dad's part, but oh well. He's always been a man of few words.

16. Jealousy Can Eat Even the Best People

Not to make it sound like Matt's career was ever in a slump, but things were really looking up now that he had that Cole Collins' audition coming up. Life is good.

I am so excited for tonight. Matt, Lilly, and I are attending a Make-A-Wish fundraiser down at the Hilton Hotel in Beverly Hills. Matt had invited Grace, but she couldn't come because her boss was making her attend a meeting up in Santa Monica with him. So sadly, tonight was not the night I would meet the mysterious Grace.

I'm especially excited because Lilly and Matt are going to be operating a kissing booth with Magdalene Jule. This wasn't originally *their* job, the other two spots were supposed to be for Channing Tatum and Amanda Seyfried, but they both had to suddenly cancel. And even though it makes sense that Matt is doing the kissing booth because he's a celebrity, you might be wondering why Lilly is. Well, let's just say, I pulled a few strings to make my germ cautious friend have to kiss strangers. But it's all for a good cause, right? I mean, every kiss is a dollar and seeing Lilly isn't a celebrity she may not even have to kiss anyone.

The doorbell rings and I let Lilly in; we planned we would get ready together here at my house. In her hands is huge make-up bag, curling iron because she isn't lucky enough to have natural ringlets like me, and a canvas dress bag.

"Hey," she said breathlessly like she had just ran a marathon, puh-leese, I could see her mom's car backing up from where she dropped her off. That's like 10 feet, but she was carrying like 60 pounds of beauty supplies.

"Need a hand?" I asked as I grabbed the curling iron and make-up bag from her hands, "Geez! What is in this bag? A brick?"

"Right," Lilly replied as we made our way up the staircase. Once we got in my room she laid the dress bag on my bed and unzipped it revealing a fun, white, knee-length Gucci dress with cut outs. "Don't you love it?" Lilly piped.

"I *love* it," I imitated her in the same girly tone.

"Thanks! I was thinking of pairing it with that Tiffany key necklace I have and my Miu Miu peep toes, you know? Do you think that would work?"

"Totally."

"Let me take a look-see at your dress!" Lilly clapped her hands excitedly.

"Ok," I'm so excited about my dress. Supposedly Taylor Swift has the same one. It's a strapless Vera Wang Lavender Label orange, knee-length dress with a cute flower detail on the neckline that I decided I'd pair with a few different strands of Chanel necklaces and Steve Madden heels. The outfit took me ages to put together, but it was so worth it.

When Lilly lays eyes on my outfit she immediately says, "You will look so gorgeous."

"Aw, you will too," we give each other a quick hug, "On to hair and make-up?" I ask her.

When we are all ready and wearing flawless make-up, we *really* do look gorgeous. Lilly decided on putting her hair into a cute French braid studded with a few pearl hairclips. I decided to leave my hair down and simple. Since I always get compliments on how beautiful my curls are I don't really like to do anything to them.

"I am so hot," Lilly jokes pretending to kiss herself in the mirror.

I scrunched my face funny and go, "You're the fire to my barbeque!"

We both erupted in laughter and make our way down to the living room where we wait for Matt. When Matt comes down only a couple minutes later I can't help but gawk at how handsome Matt really is in his Armani suit. Now if only, there was actually a boy I *could date* who dressed like him! Now I see Matt's appeal to all the other girls in the world...

For what might be the first time in his life Matt doesn't look twice at me (not that he ever does to me because I'm his sister, but still) or Lilly and how pretty we look. Wow. He really does like Grace. Even with Natalie who he thought he "really liked" he continued to give girls approving glances. Hmm, what could this mean? That Matt is *completely* serious in a relationship? Could it be?

The three of us walk out to the car where Neil, Matt's bodyguard, is patiently waiting in the driver's seat. Or rather, where I think I know he's waiting since I can barely see past the heavily tinted windows. Matt, Lilly, and I all squeeze into the backseat where I place myself as a barrier between them since I don't honestly know what terms they're on.

"Let's bounce, Neil," Matt tells Neil as Neil starts the engine.

♥♥♥

Twenty awkward minutes later (it's an uncomfortable situation being stuck between a pair of exes) we finally arrive at the resort and I practically scramble out of the car so I don't have to be in such a close proximity of both Lilly and Matt at once. I take a deep breath, breathing in some fresh air or rather fresh-as-California-air-gets-with-all-the-smog-air.

"I'm so happy to be here! Aren't you happy to be here, Matt?" I gush.

"Yeah, sure, listen, can we get inside?" Matt asks, already being led by Neil through a crowd of media and uninvited fans.

Lilly and I smile for the magazine photographer even though we know that we aren't supposed to like them "bugging us." Let's face it, what high school girl doesn't want to appear in a nationwide magazine looking really beautiful for all her classmates to see? I know that I have no problem with it.

Once we meet Matt and Magdalene at the kissing booth and I guiltily ask Magdalene for a picture and autograph, a Make-A-Wish volunteer hands Lilly, Magdalene, and Matt each a little heart covered flower vase for the kissing money. She tells them to feel free to kiss people on the cheeks if that's all they feel comfortable doing. For about the first 10 minutes at the booth we simply sit and wait for people to arrive since we came early. During this time, I scurried around to get them all a drink and ask the volunteer for Chap Stick for Matt because unlike Lilly and Magdalene he does not wear shimmery, berry colored lip gloss.

When I finally finish all of this, the lines start to form. They all kissed a couple of adorable babies' heads and Make-A-Wish kids. Otherwise Matt's line was jam packed with flustered teen girls and Magdalene's of nervous teen boys. Lilly, actually, had a relatively long line of boys herself. Apparently, she looked a lot like one of the Abercrombie models. A little uncalled for, but works for me, that just means she has to kiss more people. Ha.

The whole kissing booth process had been running pretty smoothly for about an hour and a half, until there was a dilemma at an hour and 31. Alexa had reached the front of Matt's line for a kiss. How could this have happened? I hadn't even seen her get in line, let alone arrive. And, *why* did this happen? Why was Alexa asking for a kiss from Matt, her ex, the boy who broke her heart?

So when she appeared seductively in front of Matt and placed her dollar in the flower vase, you can imagine all of our confusion. Even Magdalene was puzzled.

"Hey Matt," Alexa smiled sweetly and spoke casually as if she asked her exes for kisses all the time.

"Alexa?" Matt asked in disbelief, "What are you doing here?"

"Getting my kiss for charity, what does it look like I'm doing?" Alexa looked at Matt like he had just asked her the most ridiculous question ever.

"Oh," Matt blinked, still confused, "Wait, I'm sorry, do you mean a kiss from Magdalene or something? Because..." Matt left his thought unfinished and continued to stare at Alexa like she was a mermaid or something equally as unlikely.

Alexa rolled her eyes and flipped her hair over her shoulder. She said nothing.

"Alexa," I stared in utter confusion, "Why are you *really* here?"

"Omigosh, will it take a hammer to put it into your guys' heads that I am just getting a kiss for charity?" Alexa asked impatiently.

"But, Alexa..." Matt went on, but was forced to stop when Alexa bent over to where he was sitting, put her hands on the sides of his face, running her perfectly manicured fingers through his hair, and kissed him softly for what felt like ages. But, I realized, with immense pride in my brother, who always raved how he loved Alexa's kissing, he was not kissing her back.

"Alexa," Matt mumbled, pushing her back lightly, "I...I can't do this. I think I've finally changed, I mean, before I met Grace I probably would have totally and completely given in to that, but not now. I'm sorry Alexa, I just can't do this." OMG my little Matty was growing up!

Alexa used her flawless acting skills and pretended to not know what Matt was implying about their kiss, "I don't understand what you mean."

"Yes, you do." Matt assured her calmly.

"But, but, you kissed all those other girls," Alexa frowned.

"Alexa, you know this was different, you had some sort of separate motive." Matt made a gesture as if to motion to the air around them.

"But, you cheated on me," Alexa whispered almost inaudibly.

Matt shook his head, "And I'm really, really, really sorry for that. I really am, that was cruel of me and I know what that put you through. Therefore, I'm asking you not to try to make me do the same thing to Grace."

Alexa sighed and looked at Matt with a cross between understanding, sadness, and betrayal in her eyes. She opened her mouth to say something, but decided against it and simply walked away.

"Well," I managed to say, so much was running through my mind: Matt's beautiful speech, Alexa showing up, Matt pointing out how he had lost his girl craziness, Alexa showing up, Matt hinting at his feelings for Grace, Alexa showing up...what just happened?

"Well," Lilly and Matt both said after me.

Magdalene blinked and sighed, "Well, I guess this just shows that jealousy can eat even the best people."

We all nodded in agreement.

17. What Happened In There?

Magdalene's right. Jealousy can consume anyone, even the sweetest girls, like Alexa. The minute I recovered from my shock I ran around desperately trying to find Alexa, leaving the others inside manning the kissing booth. When I finally found her, she was crying in front of the mirror in the ladies room next to the entrance to the ballroom.

"Alexa?" I walked up to her, tapping her on the shoulder, "What happened in there?"

"I'm so sorry, Carolyn. I'm so, so sorry. I don't know what came over me...I almost did to Grace what...I don't know what happened," Alexa sobbed.

"Sweetie, I love your honesty and I do accept your apology, but it isn't me you have to apologize to. Matt's really thrown off! I can't believe you did that to him...I mean, Alexa, I'm sorry you're going through this and all, and as a friend I want to cry with you, but as Matt's sister I can't believe you would put Matt through that. He's confused with his feelings for Grace as it is." I told Alexa as I went to take my arm from her shoulders.

I turned to look at her, "You need to tell him you're sorry."

"And, I will, but not now. Not now, Carolyn. I just can't face him yet; I'm too embarrassed." Alexa put her head in her hands and then raised it, blinking rapidly.

I sighed, not to sound cold, but I was a little disappointed in Alexa. I mean, she's one of my best friends and I can't believe she just did that. I don't get it, one minute she hates Matt's guts, and then she tries to kiss him? What the hell?

"Ok," I gave her a quick pat on the back, "Well don't go feeling so sorry for yourself, this night's for charity, remember?"

When I met a still confused Matt, Lilly, and Magdalene back at the booth, they were just closing it up, chattering about the events that had unfolded just recently.

"You're back," Magdalene exclaimed, "Geez, what was that? What was she thinking? Did you talk to her? What did she say?" Magdalene fired at me with questions.

"I honestly have no idea, she wasn't really doing a good job at explaining." I turned to Matt then back to Lilly and Magdalene, "Can we be alone really quick?"

Lilly looked at me curiously, naïve as ever, "Why?"

"Lilly," I snapped, "Can you just go away?"

Lilly made a face, but proceeded to walk away with Magdalene. I returned my attention to Matt, "How are you doing?"

Matt shook his head, "I don't understand. Alexa always acts like she hates me and during kissing scenes in *Ignorance is Bliss* she acts as if kissing me is the last thing on the planet she'd ever want to do."

I looked towards the ceiling as if it would provide me all the answers. "I agree, Matty. I don't know either," I looked at him, trying to tell him through my expression that I felt just as confused as him.

"Well," Matt put on a forced grin, "I guess no one, not even Alexa, can resist my utterly amazing looks," Matt tried to laugh.

I smiled, "You know it," I gave him an awkward hug, expecting him to pull away, but he didn't. Instead he hugged me back.

18. The Best Medicine

Neil dropped Matt and me off at our house a little before 11:30 p.m. On the car ride home, Matt and I had planned to spend the rest of the night watching movies and stuffing our faces with Hot Tamales candy. We decided tonight would be just a night of fun to get Matt's mind off of Alexa.

The minute we stepped inside, we both ran up to our rooms to change out of our dress clothes. I changed into my favorite bright pink Juicy Couture terrycloth tracksuit. I put on my fuzzy Winnie the Pooh slippers and pulled my long ringlets into a loose pony tail. I quickly washed my face, shedding off my foundation, lip gloss, eyeliner, and mascara. When I plopped down on the couch beside Matt, who was wearing the same Old Navy tee from last night and some plaid pajama pants from the Gap, I saw he already had *Iron Man* running in the DVD player. On the table he had our other movies for the night stacked up: *Failure to Launch, Ferris Bueller's Day Off, The Proposal, Anchorman, Sherlock Holmes*, and *Date Night*. Also on the table were Hot Tamales, popcorn, and a few cans of Dr. Pepper.

Matt reminds me a lot of Tripp from *Failure to Launch,* afraid to settle down and afraid to get hurt. But, with the right girl and the right dates, Matt could really end up falling for a girl. Like Tripp, Matt might want to end up terminating the relationship the minute he realizes *how* much he really likes a girl and she likes him. I would need to prevent this from happening with Grace. I can't let Matt keep running away from his feelings. Unlike Tripp's friends, I won't lock Matt and Grace in a room together to express their true feelings and spy on them with video cameras, but I would think of something.

19. Beach Etiquette

"CAROLYN, PHONE!" Matt shouted at me from his room.

"WHY DON'T YOU GET IT?" I shouted back.

"UM, BECAUSE I'M CHANGING? DO YOU WANT ME TO RUN THROUGH THE HOUSE NAKED?"

"YOU WOULDN'T HAVE THE GUTS."

"OH, REALLY? WATCH M—"

"WILL ONE OF YOU PLEASE JUST GET THE PHONE?" our mom shouted from down in the office.

"FINE, I'LL GET IT," I exclaimed. "Martin residence."

"Hi," a girlish voice said through the phone, "Is Matt there?"

My heart stopped, oh no, was Matt cheating on Grace? Was this Grace? Who was this?

"Um, may I ask who's calling?" I asked sweetly.

"Oh, sure, sorry, this is Grace."

Even though I heard Grace perfectly, I pretended not to, wanting to talk longer, "I'm sorry who?"

"Grace, this is Grace, his girlfriend."

Ooh, I wasn't aware Grace was up to girlfriend status! Ooh! I wonder if I can find out more…

"Oh yes, yes. And why are you calling, dear?" I asked, pretending to be mom.

"Um, I'm sorry, but may I ask who this is?" Grace sounded annoyed by all my questions, "I just want to speak to Matt, please."

"Oh, yes dear! This is Matt's mother! But you can call me Hailey, that's my name; I hate being called Mrs. Martin. It makes me sound so old!" Boy, I was really nailing my mom's personality!

"Ok, Mrs. Martin, I mean Hailey; it's been nice talking to you but can I just speak to Matt now?"

"Sure honey," I cooed, "*Matty*?" I sung, covering the receiver, "It's Grace!"

"Coming," Matt yelled as he came bounding into my room and yanked the phone from my hands, "Hello? Oh hey, Grace."

I smiled to myself and went skipping into my parents' room to grab the phone. I clicked the talk button so I could listen in on Matt and Grace's conversation.

"Hi Matt," Grace was saying, "Your mom asks a lot of questions."

"My mom?" My breath caught hoping Matt wouldn't rat me out, "Oh yeah, she does. She can be pretty annoying sometimes." *Phew*, I'm safe.

Grace went on happily, "So have you thought about the beach at all?"

"Yes, I have. When should I pick you up?" Matt asked her.

"Um…how about Noon? Would that be ok?"

"Sure thing. Is there anything special I should bring?"

"Nope, I'll bring lunch and towels so we're all good," Grace said casually.

"Ok then, I'll see you at noon."

"See you then." Grace hung up the phone and I waited until Matt did the same. Then I scrambled to get into my room before Matt noticed I had left.

Just as I jumped on my bed and had grabbed a *Teen Vogue*, Matt strode in. "Sure," I said sarcastically, "Don't bother to knock, I might have been dancing around naked, but I'm sure you're used to that."

"Right, so," he asked skeptically, "why are you reading an issue of *Teen Vogue* from last September?"

Oops, "Um, I'm already planning some of the outfits I want to buy for school this year," I improvised.

"Ok, we'll go with that. So anyways, in the future can you not pose as Mom on the phone and then proceed to listen in on my *private* conversations."

"It's not like you were talking about your secret fears, you were just planning a trip to the beach."

"So you aren't denying it?" Matt joked, "You know, I could probably find a way to sue you for stalking me."

I laughed, "I'm sure you could," I paused, "So, girlfriend, huh? Isn't that a little serious for you?"

"I have had girlfriends before you know."

"No, Matt, you've had girls you go out on a date with and then kiss a few times, like Natalie. That's more of a friend who's a girl who just happens to be into you, not a girlfriend. There is a difference."

"Pssh," Matt waved my comment away like a speck of dust, "Whatever. So do you think I should wear my neon colored Billabong swimsuit or my navy and white Polo swimsuit?"

"Polo," I said, "Billabong swimsuit is way too abstract in my opinion. Personally I think the Polo is far more attractive. The Polo swimsuit says I'm-hot-but-don't-care which makes you seem even hotter, whereas the Billabong one screams I'm-hot-and-hope-all-the-girls-notice."

"Do you think the Billabong one really says that?" Matt looked at me.

"Well that may be a bit of an exaggeration, but basically," I shrugged.

"Ok then, we'll do the Polo."

I smile triumphantly, "Awesome."

♥♥♥

Is it possible to have an illness where you are too nosy about your brother's love life? Because if there is, I so have it.

I just pulled up at Laguna Beach with Lilly, who I dragged along with me, where we are going to spend the afternoon spying on my brother's date with Grace. I'm wearing my favorite bright pink Aeropostale bikini and I made Lilly wear the super cute navy blue Nautica bikini her aunt bought her while she was vacationing down in Orlando. For some reason, Lilly has refused to wear it up until now, but I was able to convince her to wear it when I lied that navy swimsuits prevent sunburns. As if.

Another reason I dragged Lilly along, asides from me wanting company, is so we could have her mom drive us since neither of us can, or at least can legally. I hopped out of Mrs. Thomas' white BMW X5 and thanked her again for driving us. For the umpteenth time she told Lilly and me to meet her in front of the parking lot at 5:00 p.m. And, for the umpteenth time we assured her we would.

"Bye girls! Have fun! Be safe!" Mrs. Thomas called in her New York accent from the car as we made our way down towards the water.

"Bye Mrs. Thomas!" I yelled sweetly back trying to embarrass Lilly even more.

Lilly waved once more, not saying a word, and we headed towards an empty patch of sand to lay down our towels. As Lilly laid our towels down and I began to apply sunscreen, I searched the perimeter for Matt and Grace. I easily found them a little ways to our left, just slightly closer to the water. Matt was wearing black Ray-Bans and a Duke hat he had purchased shortly after he learned Grace attended college there. Grace looked ready for a lazy day at the beach in a white bikini that complimented her glowing skin and had her hair pulled back into a sloppy ponytail.

I saw that Neil had a lawn chair set up just a little behind them and was wearing a Hawaiian shirt and khaki shorts along with his typical aviator sunglasses and earpiece. Even when he wasn't in a suit, Neil still managed to look intimidating.

"I still don't understand why you insist on spying on Matt and Grace's date," Lilly said in an irritated tone.

"Well, Miss Snappy-pants, you're just no fun," I turned to her and shrugged, "Besides, it's not like I'm able to hear them. I just wanted to see them in action."

"That's what she said," Lilly said smugly.

"Oh, just get your mind out of the gutter." I retorted back.

Lilly crossed her arms and lay down, "Whatever, I'm going to work on my tan, have fun stalking."

I wacked Lilly's belly then walked towards the ocean. When I dipped a light pink painted toe into the water I shivered. Like just about every day of the year, the California ocean was chilly. Oh well. I daintily submerged myself into the water and reemerged covered in goose bumps, but unwilling to get out. I swam around, keeping my eye on Matt and Grace. They were talking and then laughing in short bursts. I was surprised when Matt began to apply sunscreen on Grace's back, but caught up in the clichéd summer romance of it all. As Matt rubbed in the thick sunscreen, Grace began to tell him a long, and what must have been funny by the way Matt was chuckling, story. When she finished her story, Matt finished with the sunscreen and they began to kiss gently with Grace still sitting in front of Matt. So adorable!

Throughout the date, I alternated between watching the two from my towel and the ocean. Lilly tanned the whole time except for when she got up to reapply sunscreen and use the restroom. It was a sweet thing to watch, their date, they just spent the hours enjoying each other's company, laughing, and sharing little kisses. I was so jealous. I want to go on a date like that!

For most of the date, people let Matt be, but towards the end more girls noticed his presence so Matt agreed to sign a few harmless autographs and take a few pictures with blushing girls. Otherwise, people left him alone, and Matt was blessed with not being surprised by the appearance of any annoying paparazzi. Even though, with the smile Matt and Grace had on their faces, I don't think either of them would have minded having their picture taken together for the entire world to see.

20. Misunderstandings

"Lilly, you really should have stayed up and watched the date with me; it was like a scene from an adorable romance movie!" I gushed.

Lilly, who was ending up spending the night at my house, didn't seem convinced, "You don't say?"

"It was so sweet! They didn't even have a make-out session which is so unlike Matt. They just sat there and shared stories and laughs and, aw, Lilly it was so cute!" I continued to gush like a preteen girl.

"Cool," Lilly replied absentmindedly picking at her bright purple nails.

I put my *Glamour* magazine down, "Lilly, what's your deal? You're not acting like yourself tonight. When Matt was dating Natalie just a week and a half ago you would stay up all night talking about this stuff with me! What's wrong?"

Lilly looked at me like I was missing a major detail, "I didn't mind talking about Matt and Natalie because I was pretty sure that Matt wasn't actually serious about her and had convinced myself that I still had a chance. But with Grace it's different. I can tell he is COMPLETELY into her. He didn't even give me a second glance before the Make-A-Wish thing! I have like no chance with him now that he's with Grace."

I blinked, taking it all in, "But, you didn't seem to mind the other day before your highlights. By the way, you're hair looks the same, guess I was right about you not needing highlights," I added smugly.

"My appointment was cancelled!" Lilly gave me the same look that she had earlier, "Because I hadn't realized that when you said that he really liked her you actually meant that he really, *really* liked her. So I brushed it aside and decided you didn't mean anything." Lilly shrugged, "I guess I was wrong."

"Oh," was all I could think of to say. I couldn't believe even Lilly was jealous of Grace. Next thing I know all of Matt's ex girlfriends and "girls who are friends and who just happened to be into him" will show up telling me they're jealous of Grace, too! Maybe Matt's feelings for Grace were more enviable (is that even a word?) than I had first understood.

21. Audition Day

Magdalene called last night asking Matt if he wanted a ride to his Cole Collins's audition since she had to attend anyway to run scenes with him. I couldn't help but tell as I listened in on their phone call (yes, I listened to Matt's call again, but if people don't like that they should stop calling the house phone) that Magdalene sounded a little too bubbly. Could I even say flirtatious? No bother, she *was* the one who pointed out what jealousy could do to people, so I'm sure she has it all under control, right?

A little earlier today, Magdalene came to pick Matt up. She pulled up to our large house in a shiny red Lexus SC 430 convertible and had dramatically removed her purple framed Bvlgari sunglasses. Observing from my bedroom window, I watched as she rang the doorbell, texting whoever (maybe supermodel Karlie Kloss who is supposedly her BFF) as she waited, and when Matt answered, briefly stepped inside.

Then, I ran to the top of the stairs so I could watch them inside. They said their pleasantries and Matt offered her water while he got his script from the kitchen. It was really very boring, nothing scandalous or even remotely exciting, so I found myself glad when they left for the audition.

Now I sit here, bored out of my mind, just five minutes after they left wishing I could know what they're doing. Obviously they were driving to the audition but I wondered what they were talking about.

My friends at school think I'm addicted to drama. I'd love to say that they're wrong. I'd love to tell them that I'm just so accustomed to drama it's just as if I've grown attached to it, but I can't say that. I really do love drama, or maybe love isn't the right word. It's more of a love-hate thing, I hate drama in my circle of friends, but I can't help, but be interested in my brother's dramatic love life.

I've been ignoring Alexa lately. I just don't want to deal with her whining. So far, Alexa alone has filled up my voicemail with 31 messages and sent me 34 text messages in the couple of days since the kissing booth incident. She needs to figure out that I'm not the one she needs to apologize to or just stop complaining about the thing, *she* caused, completely.

ALEXA'S MOBILE: Carolyn, please call/text me back. Idk if you're mad, sad, or your phone is dead. Please forgive me!!! xo Alexa ☹

Make that 35 text messages.

♥♥♥

At 4:00 p.m. I was lounging contently on the couch eating a caramel Ghirardelli chocolate square, watching another recorded episode of *Glee* when Matt walked in.

"Hey," I greeted him, hitting pause on the TV, "How'd it go?"

Matt kicked off his shoes and placed his hands behind his head, "Good. I think I may have gotten the part." He paused, "Want to hear about it?"

"Sure." I nodded.

"Ok, so when I got in Magdalene's car she began to go on and on about her love for *Ignorance is Bliss* and would not shut up for the entire car ride. So when we arrived at the studio you can imagine my happiness..."

♥♥♥

Matt and Magdalene made their way to Stage 3 in the Cole Collins' Productions Studio and were surprised to be greeted by Cole Collins himself who was serving as the casting director. Or at least, Matt was surprised.

"Matthew Martin," Cole took Matt's hand in his, shaking it roughly, "Pleasure to meet you."

"Um, yes," Matt struggled to find the right words, "you too, Mr. Collins, but it's just Matt."

"Not Matthew?" Cole inquired, "But Matthew is such a good, Christian name!"

Matt had no idea how to respond so instead asked, "So where do I start?"

"Oh yes, yes the audition," Cole went to sit at a wooden table covered in papers, "you can begin right there." He pointed to the front right corner of the stage, "Maggy, how about you two do a run through of Scene 8?"

"Sure," Magdalene chirped and pulled her script from her oversized Hermes tote, without even bothering to correct the fact he called her Maggy.

When they had both quickly reviewed the scene they set down their scripts and Magdalene began, "So, Wilson if you want to see me again maybe we could have dinner sometime. Just a suggestion," Magdalene stood up gathering her things.

"Wait!" he called as she began to walk away, "Erin!"

Magdalene (aka Erin) turned back to him, tilting her head and asking coyly, "Yes?"

"Did you want to maybe grab something to eat tonight?" Matt asked hopefully.

Magdalene bit her lip, "Hmm, sorry, tonight doesn't work for me; I have a date with someone."

Matt (aka Joe) pretended to be aghast, "Who? You just told me we should get together for dinner sometime, I mean that seems as if that implies you aren't dating anyone!" Matt shook his head.

"Oh yeah, sorry I forgot to mention I was with someone," Magdalene smiled as if she held a juicy secret, "He's a really great guy. Tall, blonde, handsome, great sense of humor, you'd love him."

"What's his name?"

"I'm sure you could figure that out for yourself...or I could tell you. Hey, how about I tell you tonight over dinner? I know my date doesn't have plans yet."

"Wait, what? I thought you had dinner plans tonight with..." Matt trailed off and then realization washed over his face, he grinned.

Magdalene winked and as she continued to walk away, added, "I'll see you at 7 tonight at Jill's Café."

Cole clapped furiously as they wrapped up the scene, "Perfect! I love it! Matt you've found yourself a part in this movie as Joe."

Matt nodded enthusiastically, "Thank you. Thank you so much Mr. Collins. You won't be disappointed."

"I better not be." Cole returned to a businesslike tone, "We begin shooting beginning of August, so in about 6 weeks, probably up near Napa Valley; I'll be sending out an email soon and your contract."

"That's great, Matt! Congratulations!" Magdalene squealed and she hugged him with her arms around his neck.

Matt was caught off guard and gently attempted to push Magdalene away only to find her lips beginning to kiss the side of his neck. She kissed him softly, just little pecks, her lips only seeming to brush the warm skin of his neck. Matt was so stunned, frozen, and she quickly made her way to his lips, with her mouth slightly open, pulling his arms around her waist.

"Mr. Collins," a girl's voice said, "I have Meryl Streep's contract for--- Matt?"

Magdalene stopped kissing Matt abruptly and Matt took a few steps away, "Grace?" Matt gasped.

Grace blinked, "What the--- Mr. Collins, I'm sorry, I know this isn't my business, but was this," she gestured towards Matt and Magdalene, "part of a scene?"

"No, we had just finished up with Scene 8, but," he smiled wistfully, "that, that was really something! You two have more chemistry then I could ever imagine! This is fantastic! You two won't even need a call back! Not that I do call backs that often, really they're overrated..." Cole trailed off.

"Grace, I promise you that wasn't what it looked like! She," Matt pointed to Magdalene accusingly, "kissed me! You have to believe me."

Magdalene's hand shot to her mouth, "Oh my, is that your girlfriend?" she asked Matt in a hushed voice.

Grace crossed her arms furiously. "You better believe it is," she said curtly then turned back to Matt, "Jesus, Matt! What are you a girl magnet? Now, maybe once, I get it. Alexa's wrapped up in jealousy and can't control herself. We're all human, people make mistakes," she shook her head, "but twice? With some girl you've never even mentioned being romantically...involved? Matt, I'm having some trouble seeing it as just being the fact that girls can't help but fall for you. I don't know what you're doing, but if it's trying to make me consider breaking up with you, it sure as hell is working!"

"Grace? Please try to understand," Matt said helplessly.

Grace threw up her hands, "Understand what, Matt? That two girls so far have tried to hook up with you during our relationship?"

"Hey," Magdalene cut in, "I was *not* trying to hook up with him."

"Whatever, I don't care what your intentions were, but bottom line, you were kissing *my boyfriend*, and you," Grace glared at Matt, "did not seem too intent on stopping her."

22. Girl Troubles

"...so after Grace stormed out of the studio," Matt continued, "I told Cole that I'd see him when we began shooting, if not sooner, and chased Grace out of the room. But, of course, she had already left so I called Neil and had him bring me home instead of Magdalene." Matt sighed, "So that was my day."

I took a moment to process, then smacked my lips in thought, "Well," I began, "I think you got the part. That's good."

"Wow, really Carolyn? How did you figure that out?" Matt looked at me.

Despite myself, I grinned, "I'm a genius like that."

Matt chuckled, "Indeed you are, now, what are we going to do? About all my girl troubles, that is."

I looked at him, feigning shock, "We? I'm sorry, but you're the one being fought over. I'm, I'm just your innocent, sweet little baby sister."

"Ha. Ha. Sure you are." Matt retorted, "Seriously, Carolyn help me here. You're a girl; try to relate to them, what they're feeling. What could I do to turn Alexa and Magdalene off, but Grace back on?"

"Well, as you so cleverly pointed out, I obviously am a girl. But, unlike those girls, I was never nearly as stupid enough to fall for someone with as many relationship problems as you," I paused.

"Ok, so what could we---wait, excuse me, I do not have relationship problems," Matt fumed.

I smiled at my clever dig and went on, "So here's what we could do."

23. Homemade Lemonade

I was crouched around a nearby corner watching Matt as he nervously rang the doorbell of Alexa and her sister's loft. He glanced back at my corner nervously.

"It's fine," I mouthed, "She's home." I glanced back at my phone to make sure I read the text correctly.

MY MOBILE: hey what's up?

ALEXA'S MOBILE: just hanging at home...on my 2nd pint of cookie dough ice cream...wbu?

Matt shook his head and turned back to face the clean pinewood door, drumming his fingers on his Lacoste short covered thighs. Finally, after what seemed like ages, Alexa's sister answered the door.

"Hi Matt," Monica said icily, "What are you doing here?"

Matt plastered on a big smile, "I came to see Alexa. Hi Monica, you look pretty today."

I chuckled from behind my corner. Sure, Monica herself *was* strikingly pretty, but her outfit? Not so much. Judging by her large "I ♥ NY" tee and her pink plaid pajama shorts, she had just awoken from bed, at least she managed to brush her hair and swipe on some lip balm before she answered the door. And, hello, it's called wearing sunscreen which by taking a glance at her slightly peeling shins she had forgotten to apply last time she went tanning.

Despite herself Monica blushed, "Thanks. Um...Alexa should be in her room, do you want to come in?"

"Yes, thank you."

"Yeah, sure," Monica said leading him in the house, obscuring my view. I could barely make out their conversation, "Did you want --- to drink?"

"Do --- have Sprite?" Matt asked.

"Is lemonade ok?" I heard Monica say.

"Perfect."

After, I assume, Matt was poured his lemonade, Monica called Alexa, "Lexa? Matt's here to see you! I'll leave --- alone." Monica told Matt.

"Thanks," Matt told Monica, silence, "Hello Alexa, it's nice to see you."

"Mmhmm. So what is it you're here for?" Alexa asked with a slight edge in her voice.

"I wanted --- tell you that I don't have --- for you. I really like Grace and the whole kissing thing sort of jeopardized --- relationship, but I really like you, too.

But not like that, not in a romantic way. I know this is the cheesiest thing to say, but it's true, can we just be friends?"

Bam, right there, Matt's got her. No one likes the "can we just be friends" line. Even if a boy and girl stay friends the line always seems to serve as a temporary way to crush any romantic feelings.

"I guess --- can do that." Alexa replied.

"Thanks. Hey, this is amazing lemonade. Where can I get some?"

"Monica made it." Alexa sounded irritated.

"Well, it's really great," I think Matt began to chug the rest of his lemonade. "Bye. Say bye to Monica for me."

"See you around, Matt," Alexa said and I ran back to the concealment of my corner as she opened the door and Matt walked out.

The door clicked and Matt came around my corner."How'd it go?" I asked him as we made our way out the building.

"Alexa," Matt grinned devilishly, "No longer has any romantic feelings, whatsoever, for my lemonade loving butt."

♥♥♥

As a true sign that Alexa was over Matt, a pitcher of homemade lemonade arrived for Matt the next day, but not from Alexa. Attached to the pitcher was a note that read in curly handwriting:

Matt, Alexa mentioned how you complimented my lemonade so I made you a batch. Enjoy!! ~ Monica Kipley

This was a sign that Alexa was over Matt because the lemonade was sent from Monica not Alexa. Had Alexa still been into Matt she would have forced her sister to let the lemonade be signed either just "Alexa" or "Alexa *and* Monica." Any way to squeeze her name in there and show how considerate she could be, but since the lemonade was from *Monica*, Alexa clearly no longer felt the need to impress Matt.

♥♥♥

That afternoon once Matt and I have finished devouring Monica's lemonade and texting her asking for more we decided to go pay Magdalene a little visit. Our plan of attack for Magdalene was different than the one we had used on Alexa. Matt had been confused why we didn't just do the same thing, but I had insisted that doing something completely different would be much more fun.

I hopped out of Matt's beat up (rental) Chevy Malibu which we intended to use as our somewhat, some would even say cruel, scheme. I glanced back down at my horrible outfit that I had borrowed from Lilly (Shh! She doesn't know I hate the outfit). I was wearing a cheap polyester orange button down and a God awful pair of green short-shorts with a completely unflattering zipper down the left side paired with gladiator sandals in the same shade of bright green.

Matt was wearing an equally bad outfit that he borrowed from the set which was supposed to belong to Thomas Goodwin, his redneck uncle on *Ignorance is Bliss*. It consisted of a large pair of faded denim overalls with big brass buttons over a white t-shirt along with a pair of hiking boots in a shade of brown equivalent to manure.

I skipped up to the door, my curly red hair bouncy in its highly hair-sprayed Pippy Longstocking pigtails, and rang the doorbell.

"Hello, Carolyn," Magdalene answered before her jaw nearly hit the floor, "Oh my golly dang, what the hell happened to you?"

"What?" I asked, playing innocent as if I dressed this ugly every day, "Oh, my outfit. Yeah, I got it yesterday. Isn't it adorable? It's even made of real polyester!" I said in mock astonishment.

Magdalene clucked her tongue, "I'm sorry? What? Why are you even here?"

I slapped my forehead, "Oh, right, don't worry I didn't come all the way here just to show you my outfit!"

Magdalene sighed a sigh of relief, "Ok, good," I faked an expression of hurt that she dissed my outfit and she was quick to retrace her words, "Not, not, that I don't love your outfit!" I smiled and she went on, "So why are you here?"

"Matt just got this super hot car and we wanted to know if you wanted to go for a ride with us," I said enthusiastically.

"Sure!" Magdalene began to head out the door, but I stopped her.

"Oh no, you don't! It's a surprise!" I gasped as I covered her eyes, "And don't worry, I remembered to wash my hands yesterday, or wait, did I? Gosh, I would have thought I did after helping dad put in some plants…all that dirt! No bother, a few clogged pores never hurt anyone, right?"

Magdalene wrinkled her nose, "You know you don't need to cover my eyes, I swear I won't peek!"

"No! That would ruin the fun, silly!" I chirped, keeping my hand over her eyes as I led her to Matt's "super hot car" and then ripping my hand off her eyes I squealed, "Ta-da! Isn't it pretty? I picked out the color, I hear they call it Elephant Butt Gray. Don't you love it? I so love it!"

Magdalene's jaw hit the floor once again, "I have no idea what to say."

"I know!" I gushed. "I felt the same way when I first saw old Froggy the Toad here." I patted the car affectionately."That's its name, you know, Froggy the Toad. I thought of it when I first heard how the engine sounds when the car starts, it sounds just like a toad giving birth to a frog." I spoke slowly as if I was speaking to someone who speaks another language, so she would be able to process my every word.

"A toad giving birth...to a frog?" Magdalene asked me incredulously.

"Exactly, hear for yourself. Start her up Matt!" I shouted acknowledging Matt's presence for the first time.

Matt stood up plastering a goofy look on his face, "Hey, Maggy."

Magdalene took a deep breath to calm herself, "It's Magdalene."

"Oh, yes, sorry Magdalene. Like my outfit?" He asked doing a spin to show it off in all of its unfashionable glory. "I bought it yesterday when I went shopping with Carolyn. Hey, did you know Wal-Mart isn't lying about having the lowest prices? We got these outfits for quite the bargain!"

I tapped my foot, "Matt, come on, start the car!" I turned to Magdalene, "You'll love it."

"Alright, alright," Matt groaned leaning over to turn on the ignition.

VRROOMGURGORGVRROOMGURGLEGORGLE the engine roared, or should I say groaned, to life.

"Oh my golly dang," Magdalene whispered to herself before raising her voice to a somewhat concerned tone. "Hey, guys, I am so silly," she rolled her eyes in mock embarrassment, "but I have somewhere I need to be with…someone. It's not that I wouldn't love to hang out with you guys and," she gestured towards our car, "Toady the Frog—,"

"Froggy the Toad," I corrected her.

"Froggy the Toad," Magdalene went on, "but I really have to be somewhere."

"Where?" Matt asked with a wounded expression.

Magdalene waved her hands, searching for an excuse, "Somewhere...other than here. It's top secret stuff, if you know what I mean."

I nodded my head knowingly, "Ah, top secret, I know what you mean."

She furrowed her eyebrows, "You do? Oh, wait, yes you do. Well, I better get going, see you guys later!" Magdalene practically ran to the door. Once she had slammed it closed, I turned to Matt.

"I thought she would never leave. Can we go home now? I want to get out of these hideous clothes soon as possible."

"I know," Matt scrunched up his nose, "Hey, are yours kind of itchy? I feel like I'm going to break out in a rash..."

I nodded my head in agreement, "I know! I've been so itchy! I think Mom may have just bought some Aloe Vera."

"Really? I could have sworn we just ran out..."

24. Texting Typos

I was lying by the pool in my navy and white striped Tommy Hilfiger bikini lathering my tomato red torso in Aloe Vera. Matt was upstairs soaking in tomato juice. I had tried to assure him that that's only supposed to work on skunk odor, but he was convinced that it was for rashes *not* skunk odor.

On the chair besides me was Matt's BlackBerry Bold which I had stolen from him in order to text Grace.

MATTY'S MOBILE: hey, I'd like to apologize 4 kissing other girls (even though they kissed me) while we're dating...will u accept my apology? ☹

GRACE'S MOBILE: who said we were still dating??

Ouch. Come on Grace. They kissed him! Have a heart! It's tough for him to be so attractive!

MATTY'S MOBILE: I did??

GRACE'S MOBILE: hm....fine, apology accepted ☺

MATTY'S MOBILE: thanks...want 2 come over 2nite?

GRACE'S MOBILE: if u insist, I guess I can squeeze u in

MATTY'S MOBILE: fantastic! I have 2 go! bye! love you!

GRACE'S MOBILE: u love me?

Huh. I guess I should have investigated with Matt first to see if they had even exchanged "I love you" yet.

MATTY'S MOBILE: what??

GRACE'S MOBILE: u just said u loved me.

MATTY'S MOBILE: I did?

GRACE'S MOBILE: yes!!! that is so sweet!! I had wanted 2 tell u but I was nervous u wouldn't feel the same way but u do!! omg! I love you 2!! sorry I have to go, but I am so excited for 2nite!! love you!

Huh. So I just told Matt's girlfriend that he loves her. No big deal. I'm sure he tells all his girlfriends that...right?

25. Love Stinks

"Hey, Matty, I have something to tell you." I knocked on the bathroom door where Matt was taking his tomato juice bath.

"Come on in," Matt called back, "Just...try not to look."

I pulled the handle and walked into Matt's bathroom, which now smelled strongly of tomatoes, to see Matt sitting in a tub full of, indeed, tomato juice. My eyebrows rose, "How's the bath going?" I laughed.

Matt crossed his juice covered arms and frowned, "Really? Really? You came all the way in here to laugh at me? It isn't funny, Miss I've Died My Hair Six Too Many Times And It's So Fried That I'm Shedding."

I widened my eyes, "Hey, do you want me to leak pictures of you soaking in tomato juice to the press? I'm sure *Seventeen* would just love to do an article on you. "Matt Martin's Age Defying Remedy: Turn to Page 71 to See More!" Ooh, and then maybe we could get you something with *Allure* too! "Martin's Tomatoes: How You Can Stay Beautiful for Less!" But, with *People* and *InTouch*, for example, it could end up going differently. "Matt Martin: Could He Really Be A Tomato Addict?'"

"Oh, well, listen here---," Matt began before I cut him off. I did not come up here to bicker.

I waved my hands, "Sorry, listen, Matt, as much as I'm enjoying this conversation I have something more important to tell you about."

"Oh, I get it, you're just scared I might bring up your mustache next!"

"I do *not* have a mustache," I said firmly.

Matt lifted his hands, "If you say so. But, sure you don't want to make sure? I have a mirror."

I huffed, "Fine. Can I see the mirror?"

"Sure, it's in my jeans' pocket...no, the jeans on the *floor*."

I kneeled down; a little disgusted about reaching into the pocket of jeans Matt had just worn, and pulled out the mirror, "Wait, you have a *compact mirror*?"

Matt pouted, "I need something to check my hair," he said guiltily.

I rolled my eyes, laughing, and then checked in the mirror, "Hey, I don't have a mustache," I said reaching to wipe my upper lip, "that was foam from my Root Beer!"

Matt erupted in laughter, "I know, you didn't seriously believe me did you?" I crossed my arms at him, "Ha! You did believe me!"

"It is not funny," I huffed, "besides I have something more important to talk to you about."

♥♥♥

"You told her I loved her?!" Matt shouted.

I scratched the back of my neck, nervously, "Well, I didn't exactly verbally tell her…"

"Oh? You didn't, did you?" He raised his perfectly shaped eyebrows.

"Not exactly," I replied in a small voice, I paused, nervous to go on, "Well…I stole your phone."

Matt frowned, by far, his phone was one of his most prized possessions, "You stole my phone?"

"Yes," I replied meekly, "I stole it so I could text Grace for you."

"You posed as me? You posed as *me* so you could text *my* girlfriend?" Matt said quietly, I could detect a hint of disbelief in his tone.

"Yes," I nodded.

"So what did she say?" He asked me trying (and failing) to keep calm. It was all going to be ok. I only told his girlfriend that he loved her. I only made him take one of the biggest steps a boy can take in a relationship. I had it *all* under control.

"See for yourself," I handed Matt the phone.

Matt read through the text messages then said to no one in particular, "She said she loved me too? She loves me." Matt shook his head, confused.

"Well, the question is, Matty...do you love her?"

26. Love, Hugs, and Kisses

Grace apparently seemed like the kind of girl (even though she had insisted she wasn't when she and Matt first met) who, once convinced a guy was fully committed to a relationship, she was free to let go of all her rules and morals.

When she arrived at my house at 7 p.m. to find it was only me and Matt home, she had seemed almost giddy about the "no parents" thing. She was dressed in a seashell pink summer dress with a low neckline and Toms wedges. So this was what the famous Grace looked like up close. After all, one can only tell so much from behind bushes, spying on dates.

"Hey," Grace smiled at me warmly; revealing perfectly aligned teeth, obviously Mommy and Daddy had paid good money on her dental work.

"Hi," I smiled back at her, glad I had bothered changing out of my swimsuit and washing my hair, "You here for Matt?" I asked as if the answer wasn't already obvious, pointing behind me.

"Yeah, I'm Grace, his girlfriend." She scanned me over, taking me into account, seeing if I was competition, no doubt. If only she realized I was Matt's sister.

"Come on in," I backed out from the door way, "So, Grace, I heard about Matt's...proclamation via text today." I paused adding, "I'm his sister, Carolyn, or I don't know, a lot of my friends call me Carrie, so you can call me that if you want," I shrugged indifferently.

"Oh, yeah," color rushed to Grace's cheeks and neck. "He told me he loved me," she said happily, like a lovesick puppy.

"Wow," I said in mock shock, "That's amazing!"

Grace sighed dreamily, "It is, isn't it?" She paused rolling her eyes like all of this was silly, even though I knew she couldn't be more pleased, "So I'm hoping tonight..." Grace left her sentence unfinished, but she didn't need to say more. I knew exactly what she was thinking.

End of this school year, my friend Joanna's, who was a junior, boyfriend told her he loved her. He showered her with compliments and wouldn't leave her side. To make it worse or better, depending on your opinion, he was a senior, heading off to the big leagues, also known as the Ivy League. Joanna was flattered someone, so mature, so handsome, so charming, was really head over heels for her.

On the last night of school, Joanna's older sister, also a senior, had party on her family's yacht. Kevin (Joanna's boyfriend) acted like an idiot and got wasted. But, he managed to still act like a gentlemen towards Joanna.

I had been talking to (or rather being talked to) by a boy who just finished 7th grade and thought he was so mature and would be able to woo all the high school girls. While he blabbed about being the star of his school's lacrosse team, I was watching Joanna and Kevin. They were sitting on one of the soft leather couches making out. Kevin was beginning to run his big, rough hands through Joanna's long red-brown hair and Joanna had her arms flung around his neck. Suddenly, Joanna stood up and placed her fingers under Kevin's chin, pulling him up playfully. When he was finally standing she flung herself into his arms and despite being drunk he caught her with lighting fast reflexes.

Joanna continued to kiss Kevin roughly, like she needed him like the air we breathe. Kevin began to carry her to the bedroom. That was the last I saw of Joanna the whole night.

A month later, Joanna called me sobbing her heart out.

"Carrie?" Joanna sobbed in a tiny voice. She had sounded so afraid, so vulnerable.

My breath caught, "Oh no, Joanna, you aren't..." I left my sentence unfinished, already knowing the answer.

"I am."

"Oh my God, Joanna, I'm so, so sorry." I cooed.

Joanna had taken a pregnancy test. When she told her parents, they were devastated. Her mother had moped around for days, insensitive to her daughter's feelings, muttering things like, "I thought we raised you right." Her dad had shown almost no emotion. He was stoic like a statue, only able to comfort Joanna with a few stiff, awkward hugs.

So, obviously, when Grace implied she wanted to do IT with Matt, I was caught slightly off guard...ok, totally caught off guard. I knew that the chance of her getting pregnant was basically 50/50 so she may luck out, she may not get pregnant...but what if she does?

"Um, Carolyn, Carolyn are you, like, there?" Grace looked at me nervously, taking me out of my trance.

"Don't forget a condom," I blurted out without thinking.

Grace blinked, "I'm sorry, what? Are you *insane*?"

My eyes widened. Oops, so that isn't what she meant. "Um, nothing sorry, that's um, an inside joke between me and…Magdalene?" I said, using the first thing I could think of.

Grace blinked again while this registered. "I'm sorry, but I think you misunderstood me, I don't want to have *that* with Matty! What do you think I am, a slut or something?"

My cheeks burned, "Omigosh, I'm *so* sorry! I don't think you're…I just….I'm sorry."

She huffed and crossed her arms, irritated, "Well, good," She began to blow past me, up the stairs, towards Matt's room, "Even if I did, you know, I wouldn't want a *child's* opinion!"

"Well, then what did you plan on doing while you were *all* alone tonight? Playing cards?" I snapped.

Grace rolled her eyes carelessly, even though I could tell I had ticked her off, "Trust me," she snapped, "I'm sure there are plenty of ways we can use the cards."

Ok, seriously, what does that even mean?

27. When They Got a Room

My mom had left pizza money for Matt and me. Matt had always been a picky eater, his likes and dislikes changing from day to day, so you could never order him something without his approval. So, I had to abandon my job of transferring my stuff from my Dooney & Bourke bag to a metallic JJ Winters bag my mom had picked up for me at a fundraiser so I could go ask Matt and Grace what kind of pizza they wanted.

I stepped up to Matt's door, "Matt?" I knocked, "What kind of pizza do you guys want?" I paused, no answer, "Matt, you in there?" I asked again, still no answer. "Fine, I'll just come on in." I said crisply.

I opened Matt's door and screamed.

"WHAT THE HELL?" I screamed, "GRACE GET OFF OF HIM! THAT IS DISGUSTING! OMIGOSH! WHAT ARE YOU DOING? I DON'T UNDERSTAND! MATT, ARE YOU OUTTA YOUR FREAKING MIND?" I shouted, utterly repulsed.

Finally noticing my presence, Matt looked up and did a double-take, "WHAT THE? CAROLYN?! WHY

ARE YOU IN HERE?" Matt yelled at me, sitting up from under Grace's seductive position.

Grace, who had somehow been unaware of our screaming, was startled by Matt's sudden movement, "Matt," she purred, "What are you doing?" Matt's face was red as a beet, "Are you feeling--- Carolyn," Grace's tone was cool as ice, "get *out.*"

Matt put up his hands, "Grace, it's all right, it isn't like she caught us doing anything pornographic or anything."

"I wouldn't be surprised if it ended up that way in a few hours." I muttered, causing Matt to shoot me the stink eye.

"But, what if she tells the paparazzi or someone? This would look horrible." Grace said uneasily.

Matt sighed, "She's my sister, why would she tell the media? So she could look like she comes from a family of careless hook ups? Second of all, according to my publicist Rebecca, no press is bad press, so even if she did, I'm sure I would survive." Matt smiled at Grace and stroked her cheek gently. He turned his head to look at me, "Pepperoni, would be great thanks," He gave me a slightly devilish grin, "Now, we would really like to get back to what we were doing so if you could leave us now we would be totally indebted."

I frowned at him, when had he become Mr. It's All Good You Only Walked in on Us Making Out?

"So, pepperoni?" I confirmed shakily.

"Yes ma'am," Matt nodded, looking over at Grace, "Now if that would be all, how about you be on--"

"And one Sierra Mist," Grace added before she resumed kissing Matt passionately.

I knew I should leave now. I should just go order the pizza, find something good on TV, and let them be, but for some reason I just had to know something.

"Grace? Why were you so nervous I would tell the paparazzi? Is it because you're honestly concerned for Matt's reputation or something else?"

Grace blinked, flushing slightly at the cheeks, "Excuse me?"

I stepped forward, pretending to be a policeman interrogating a criminal, "Were you worried someone would...find out?"

Matt snapped to attention, "About what?" He said suspiciously.

"Her little fling with Wilson Walker."

28. Walker on Sunshine

Matt's eyebrows furrowed, "Wilson Walker? As in Wilson Walker, reporter from *Gilbertson Gossip*?"

I nodded, "That's the one."

"But," Matt looked at Grace, wounded, "you *cheated* on me?"

Let me let you in on a little secret. When I first met Wilson Walker back at Alexa's movie premiere he had used himself as an example to one of the questions he asked me. Wilson had asked me if there was anything Matt typically gave to a girl he "fancied." When I had looked at him blankly he had went on to tell me how he normally gives a girl he dates a pink Brighton keychain shaped like a rose.

When Grace came in for her evening with Matt she was still carrying her car keys. While I placed them on the kitchen table for her I had noticed a pink rose keychain attached to the ring. Curious, I flipped the keychain over to see the label which was Brighton.

I had considered stomping back to Grace and handing her her keys and then demanding she leave, but decided I would confront her about it instead of assuming. However, my plan was thwarted when we got in the fight about her doing IT with Matt and playing cards. Therefore, when she acted so nervous about someone finding out about her relationship with Matt, I couldn't help my curiosity sparking.

"Matt, it's not what you think..." Grace began before letting her sentence trail off.

"Oh?" Matt fumed, "Then what the *hell* is it?"

"*Was,* Matt, *was,*" Grace insisted, her voice breaking. "It was only two dates, then it was over, the minute I realized how serious I was about you I ended it!"

I knew I should butt out, but I couldn't resist, "Then why," I barked, "do you still have the key chain on your keys?"

Grace buried her head in her hands, overwhelmed; "I just thought it was pretty!" she barked back, "Is that so wrong? That I thought it was *pretty*?"

My mind raced back to a dainty pair of cute crystal earrings Jake had given me. Grace did have a point, just because you've ended a relationship with someone doesn't mean you have to throw away things they may have given you. But, this was different, Grace *cheated* on Matt, it isn't the same as keeping something from an old boyfriend.

I looked at Grace's pleading eyes. *Please,* they said, *try to understand. I ended it, I'm innocent, I only wanted to keep the key chain.*

I softened, "Well, I guess it's ok you kept the keychain. No harm done right?" I glanced over at Matt to see him still glaring at Grace, "Matt?"

Matt's facial features softened for a split second, as if considering, before hardening again, "No, it's not ok, it's far less than ok. I cannot believe you cheated on me. With a reporter! And not just any reporter, you cheated on me with *Wilson Walker*." Matt scrunched up his nose as he said the name as if he tasted something sour, "Do you know how bad of a player that guy is? Granted, I'm no saint, but I'm sure as hell better than him!

"Dammit, Grace, I was serious about you. And not like the serious I normally think I am about girls. Like I thought with Natalie, for example, I liked her, yeah, I liked her, but I didn't *love* her. With Natalie, I still looked at girls appreciatively, I still thought, *Man, I wonder how she kisses.* But, not with you, I haven't given any girls a second glance since I started dating you. Not a second glance. I lov*ed* you." Matt coldly emphasized the past tense form of love.

Grace's eyes welled up and she mumbled softly, "Oh my, I'm so sorry Matt."

Matt closed his eyes, calming himself, "Please leave."

"What?" Grace asked, reality hitting her, "You can't be serious, Matt..."

Calmness was wiped from Matt's face and once again replaced by a sardonic expression. "I'm damn serious," he said before recovering and walking over to hold open his bedroom door. "Now, I'm sure you'll be able to find your way home just fine, have a goodnight," Matt declared,obviously trying to sound more pleasant and careless than he felt.

Grace gazed up at Matt as she stood in the doorway, throwing him one last beseeching look. "I'm so sorry, Matt," she whispered so that only Matt could hear. Then, before she finally walked out of the room, Grace stood up on her tiptoes and kissed Matt softly on the cheek.

29. Modifications and Margaritas

I was freezing. I pulled my covers higher over my head and clung tightly to my favorite stuffed animal (yes, I still sleep with one), Piggy (who, yes, is a pig). Just as I began to dose off again, and my hands began to lose circulation, I heard a soft knock on my door.

"What?" I groaned, my voice muffled from under my covers.

"It's Matt," Matt said cheerily, he'd always been a morning person, "May I come in?"

"May I go back to sleep?" I mocked him irritably.

"Not until I can come in," Matt insisted.

I heaved a heavy sigh, rolling my eyes, "Fine. Come in."

"Thank you," Matt chirped, his voice returning to its earlier pleasant tone. He opened my door, revealing the bright sunlight coming in through the halls, I groaned. "Oh, stop complaining!" Matt carped.

"What do you want?" I sat up in bed, the AC hitting my bare arms like snow, "And, make it quick," I snapped, "I'm freezing over here."

Matt chuckled, "Well, I'm on my way to a meeting regarding the Cole Collins movie---,"

"Will Magdalene be there?" I cut in.

A hint of a smile played on Matt's lips, "Yes, I think she will be. Anyways, Lilly called; apparently she has some sort of dire emergency and needs you to come over," Matt smirked.

"Ok, thanks. I'll head over soon. Hey," I paused, "how you feeling?" I bit my lip with guilt, after all in a way their split was kind of all my fault; I didn't have to tell Matt about Grace's thing with Wilson Walker. She ended it, so it's not like there was anything to tell.

Matt ignored me, "I really have to get going, and Rebecca would kill me if I was late for this meeting."

♥♥♥

Lilly's highlights and trim must have gone horribly askew because when I arrived at her house she had her hair wrapped up in a towel.

"Honey, what happened?" I asked sympathetically.

Lilly's face twisted in disgust, "See for yourself," she spat as she ripped off her towel.

My mouth formed into a tiny "o". Lilly's hair was no longer its naturally shiny platinum blonde instead it was an rather uneventful dark blonde and her "trim" had taken her hair from past her boobs so it just reached her shoulders.

Judging by Lilly's sickened expression she hated it, but I actually loved the change. Not only did her hair now perfectly frame her squarely shaped face, but Lilly could use a change. For example, she's been doing her make up the exact same way ever since I can remember (baby blue nail polish, black noir mascara, a light plum-pink blush, and her signature lavender cream eye shadow). She has also worn the same perfume since Christmas of 8th grade (Viva la Juicy). Furthermore, Lilly's been the same with her hair, since 4th grade (4th grade!) she's done her hair with a side part (always on the left side) and long layers.

"Come on now Lilly! It looks great. I love it, even more than your old color, in fact!"

Lilly shot me a displeased sneer, "Well, *I* hate it! It's so plain! So ordinary! So basic! So *unsightly*," Lilly wailed in derision.

I rolled my eyes, another thing of Lilly's that's never changed? Her attitude!

"And look how it makes my complexion look!" Lilly went on, swimming in self pity, pointing a finger at her face, "It looks so *tan*. I want alabaster, Carrie! Not tan! Alabaster!"

"First of all, Lilly, your skin is absolutely not tan. Your old hair just made it so your skin looked a little lighter, don't ask me how, but it did." I replied, "It's just a hair color, Lilly," I added haughtily, "not a major artery or something."

"But," Lilly whined, stamping her gold Fitzwell sandals stubbornly, "look at my eye shadow!" Lilly pointed at her lavender cream eye shadow indignantly, "It just doesn't look right!"

"I like your new hair Lilly," I told her calmly, running a strand between my fingers.

"Well *I* don't! And it's *my* hair!" Lilly shrieked, throwing her head in her hands.

"Then what do you want to do about it, Lilly?" I asked her impatiently. I had better things to be doing! I could be texting Grace on Matt's phone!

♥♥♥

When Lilly and I left Aveda Lilly was glowing with excitement. She bought herself a whole new stash of color preserving (Shh! she thinks they're "decolorizing") hair products and is completely convinced her new hair color will be gone in a week. I know, it was cruel of me to trick her, but she'll get over it. She always does.

Lilly and I decided to head back to my house after our Aveda shopping spree (just in case you're wondering, Lilly can legally drive now, she turned 16 a few days ago and her dad bought her a little sedan). When we walked in the door, still chatting about Lilly's new look, we were greeted by a very disgruntled Matt.

"Matt?" I asked, surprised, stopping midsentence, "Did the meeting not go well or something?"

"No, the meeting went fine, just fine, Tony---,"

"That's his agent," I whispered to Lilly.

"Yes, well, anyways Tony was able to negotiate a beyond decent pay for doing the movie," Matt continued.

"Ok," I raised my eyebrows expectantly, "so what is the problem?

"Grace was there," Matt said in abhorrence.

I clucked my tongue, "Ah."

Lilly looked from me to Matt, confused, "Wait, did you and Grace like break up or something?"

"Or something," Matt murmured before continuing, "She cheated on me," Lilly gasped, "with Wilson Walker."

"Of *Gilbertson Gossip*," I whispered to Lilly, she gasped again.

"I hate that magazine," Lilly stated crossly. "I mean, who would honestly think Jennifer Aniston's having secret meetings with Brad Pitt? Puh-leeze!"

"Anyways," Matt went on, "Grace came in during the meeting to give Cole some papers---,"

Lilly furrowed her eyebrows, "Wait, why was Grace even *there*?"

"Gracc is one of Cole Collins' assistants," I explained to Lilly.

"As I was saying, Grace came in to give Cole some papers and saw me there..."

♥♥♥

"Mr. Collins?"Grace asked, startled by Matt's presence, "May I interrupt for a minute?"

"More than you previously have?" Cole complained.

"Please, it'll only take a minute, I swear," Grace persisted.

Cole looked at the ceiling impatiently, "If you must."

"Thank you so much," Grace smiled, grabbing Matt's arm and pulling him out of the room, "Matt, we *need* to talk," Grace said adamantly.

"What if I don't want to talk?" Matt asked skeptically.

Grace put her hands on her hips and retorted back sardonically, "I think you'll survive."

"Listen," Matt snapped, "I have a *very* important meeting to be getting back to. I'm sure our little chat can wait, can't it?" Matt sneered.

"Come on, Matt," Grace began, but Matt had already closed the door behind him.

♥♥♥

"So, you just left her?" Lilly asked, perplexed, "No romantic reuniting? No dramatic passionate kisses? Not even a bitter argument?"

Despite myself, I agreed with the always romantic Lilly. "Matt that is a somewhat uneventful story. Is that all that happened? She pulled you out into the hall asking to talk to you?"

"No, of course not," Matt grunted, "Why would I waste my valuable time telling you that? I mean, I do have an interview with *Star* in like an hour.

"So after the meeting I was making my way with Tony to where Neil was waiting in the car..."

♥♥♥

"...Matt, just hear me out here. You're one of my most valued clients and I'm only doing what I think is best for you. I agree with Cole, you should pose as a couple with Magdalene in order to create more publicity for the movie," Tony advised Matt.

"Tony, I am not going to pretend to date Magdalene. There is no way. Besides, let's let my *publicist* handle my publicity, ok?" Matt patted Tony on the back triumphantly.

A loud click clacking noise began to come closer behind them and Matt turned around to face Grace, "Matt, can I please talk to you?" she pleaded.

Matt turned to Tony who had stopped his lecture, Tony shrugged and nodded.

"Can we at least go somewhere else?" Matt requested.

♥♥♥

"I don't get where you're going with this," Lilly declared. "Does this story even have a point?"

Matt opened his hands, "Do you want me to just tell you the ending?"

"No!" I cut in, "Then I wouldn't know all the details, I wouldn't know the *cause* of the *effect*."

"Then tell *her*," Matt pointed an accusing finger at Lilly, "to stop interrupting me. By the way Lilly, I like your new hair and did you do something different with your make up?" Matt was side tracked.

Lilly smiled coyly and went to twirl a lock of her hair, only to find it wasn't really long enough to twirl; she brought down her hand quickly, feeling silly.

"Oh, yeah, I did," Lilly replied, flattered but also annoyed this was the first time he noticed, "I'm glad you like it."

"Can we just get back to the story please?" I asked a little more sharply than I intended.

♥♥♥

Grace stopped her car in front of a quaint Mexican restaurant and hopped out, "You coming?" she raised her eyebrows expectantly at Matt.

Matt ignored her and stepped out of the passenger seat, "This," he asked scornfully, "is your idea of someplace else? We're not on a date you know."

Grace crossed her arms and sighed, "Whatever."

Grace got them a table towards the back of the room so they could talk without being interrupted by fans of Matt's. However, Matt couldn't help but think

Grace just wanted to be even more alone than they already were.

Matt pulled out her chair. "Always the gentleman," Grace said sardonically.

"Hey," Matt said defensively, "I'm not the one who cheated here."

Grace blushed and Matt sat in his chair. "I just wanted to say I'm sorry," Grace apologized. "I know, I've told you this like ten times, but I really feel awful." She smiled meekly.

The waiter walked by and Grace flagged him down. Matt raised his eyebrows at her drink order.

"What?" Grace snapped before biting her lip and blushing. Turning to the expectant waiter she said, "Sorry, I forgot, make that a *virgin* margarita, my mistake."

The waiter turned to Matt, "Would you like something, senor?"

"No, thank you," Matt grinned, "I don't intend on staying long." He snuck a glance at Grace to see she was frowning at his profile.

When Matt turned back to face her, she smiled, and he asked, "I'm sorry for being so rude, but is there really anything to discuss here?"

"No, but, I just want to make things right," Grace begged.

"I have to go," Matt lied, "I'm late for an appointment." Matt stood up and almost ran into the waiter carrying Grace's drink. He slipped the guy a five, "Here, this should pay for her drink." And, he walked out of the restaurant, leaving Grace all alone with her virgin margarita.

30. When Life Gives You Lemons, Lilly Makes Lemonade

"So how will you get her back?" Lilly asked Matt curiously, "Will you stand by her balcony declaring your undying love? Will you throw rocks at her window and then insist she comes and runs away with you?"

Matt and I glanced at one another and then at Lilly. Had she just missed the whole point of the story? Matt didn't want to get back together with Grace.

"Lilly, Matt doesn't want to get back together with her. She wants to get back together with him." I spoke slowly as if I was speaking to a baby, trying to make her understand.

"Oh," Lilly looked put out at the unromantic situation, but then her face lightened up, "Then, we will find a way to make Grace jealous! Put her in her place! Give her a taste of her own medicine!" Lilly declared resolutely.

Matt beamed, becoming interested in the conversation, "And how could we do that?"

"Well, first of all, we need to get you a girlfriend."

Part Four

"Pretend Princess"

Magdalene

31. Pretty Please

Lilly, Matt, and I walked up to Magdalene Jule's door and knocked simultaneously.

"I'm coming!" Magdalene called from inside, "One second!"

Magdalene opened the door, a little Beagle dancing between her feet. Her eyes narrowed when she saw us, especially Matt and me. "What?" she spat, "You here to show me another 'hot new ride'?"

Lilly glanced at me and mouthed, "What?"

I brushed Lilly's question aside, putting my finger over my mouth as a signal.

"About that…" Matt began, "Carrie and I…well, we just did that in order to ensure you wouldn't, you know…like me anymore," he blushed in embarrassment, "I guess, that was, looking back, a kind of cruel way of doing so."

Magdalene's jaw dropped, "You mean? That was all pretend? I can't believe you would do that! Why didn't you just flat out tell me?"

"Well, at the time," Matt faltered, "actually…I have no idea. It just seemed like more fun." Matt's face began to turn even more crimson as he shrugged, "Sorry."

Magdalene's features softened a bit at his apology, "Thanks, now, why are you here? Surely this is not the only reason."

Lilly cut in, "We wanted to ask you a favor."

"Do go on."

"We need you to pretend to be Matt's girlfriend. We were going to ask Monica, Alexa's sister, but we figured you would have better acting skills than her and we didn't want to risk Alexa getting jealous since we weren't going to let her in on the plan," Lilly explained rapidly.

"What if I'm still into Matt?" Magdalene asked her, exposing a flaw in our brilliant, if not slightly clichéd plan.

Matt and I, oblivious to Magdalene's sarcastic tone, looked at each other in confusement, "Wait, are you?" Matt asked, taken aback.

Magdalene laughed and scoffed, "What? No, are you crazy? After that little show you two put on?" She looked from Matt to me. "No way. I was giving you guys something to quickly brood over."

"So," Lilly piped happily, "does that mean you'll do it?"

Magdalene scratched the back of her neck, considering, "Sure. Why not? It'll be great practice for the movie, I guess, playing a couple."

Lilly beamed and reached into her oversized bohemian style bag, pulling out a purple notebook with a picture of Betty Boop on it. She handed it to Magdalene. Then she reached into her bag again and pulled out an army green notebook with an *M* on it to hand to Matt. Lilly clapped her hands giddily.

"What is this?" Matt looked at the notebook questioningly.

"Your schedules, silly," Lilly shook her head in disbelief, "I took the liberty of writing down a few dates you guys would go on. And, I'm certain that Grace will see you two lovebirds because my brother, Jeff, is friends with a close cousin of hers who was able to make a copy of her schedule for me." Lilly took a breath and in response to Matt's concerned look she continued, "Don't worry, Matt, I looked at your schedule, too, and none of these dates will pose any problems. However, I have no idea if the schedule will work for you, Maggy---,"

"It's Magdalene," Magdalene corrected her sternly.

"I mean, Magdalene," Lilly said again, "so I'm simply hoping you'll be able to make it work." Lilly smiled sweetly, "Any questions?"

32. Prepared Preparations

"You want me to wear *this*?" Magdalene asked Lilly incredulously as we zipped her into her dress the next day.

"Yep," Lilly chirped.

Magdalene looked at me uncertainly, "I don't know, guys. It seems a little bit, like, risqué don't you think?"

I took a second look at the black corset top AMI Clubwear dress and Donna Karen peep toes we had given Magdalene for her "first date" with Matt tonight which was to be at some beachside Chinese restaurant that Grace was meeting a friend at.

"Nah," I assured her, "You'll look great."

Magdalene hesitated, but then lightened up, "Oh, well, it isn't like I haven't worn anything worse, right?"

Lilly looked at me questioningly and I decided to fill her in, "Magdalene did a Broadway show last summer and there was a scene that required her to be on stage in a nude corset and panties," I smirked and added, "in a highly air conditioned room."

Lilly giggled before being silenced by Magdalene's cold stare, "So," Lilly began saying suddenly, "why don't you go get dressed," she motioned to Magdalene's huge bathroom, "and we will wait out here. Matt should be here," Lilly checked her white Chanel watch, "in about 25 minutes."

After Magdalene was dressed she did her hair in a low, loose pony tail and quickly reapplied her plum colored eyeliner. Matt arrived (ten minutes early).

I scurried downstairs to answer the door, "Helloooo?" I drawled goofily before narrowing my eyes in mock irritation. "Oh," my voice fell flat, "Matt."

"Nice to see you, too, Carrie," Matt smiled charmingly, "Is Magdalene ready?"

I glanced at my nails carelessly; I really needed a manicure, "Uh-huh." I turned my attention back to Matt, he was wearing a light yellow polo I had never seen before, and added, "Nice shirt, by the way, is it new?"

"Yeah," Matt fidgeted like he was embarrassed I noticed. "Mom dragged me down to Lacoste. She was convinced the gray one I was going to wear was 'sooo last winter'." He shrugged, "You know her."

I smiled, same old mom, "Yeah, I know what you mean. Either way though, I like it; it looks good with your hair."

Matt shook his sun bleached locks unconsciously, "Thanks." He looked towards Magdalene's room where we could hear Lilly cursing the curling iron they were trying to use to curl the bottoms of Magdalene's pony tail, "So when is she going to be ready again?"

As if on cue, Magdalene stumbled out of her room in her almost four inch heels, "Hey," she stuttered.

"Hello," Matt greeted her chivalrously, "You look pretty."

Although the date was a fake, Magdalene's cheeks turned pink, "Thanks," she came out of her trance quickly and asked, "Are you ready to go?"

"As I'll ever be," Matt responded without a hint of charisma.

Magdalene's face fell slightly, but she smiled, "Then let's go."

"Wait, wait, I have some things to tell you two," Lilly came running from Magdalene's room, carrying her Palm Pre where she kept her calendar, "When you arrive at," she glanced down at her calendar to find the restaurant's name, 'Ling's Cultural Chinese Bistro,' make sure to tell them that you spoke to Jessica on the phone and that she reserved you a booth on the balcony. If they ask, you're reserved under my last name, Thomas. And then, also, just from personal experience, do *not* try their lettuce wraps unless you like having your tongue practically burn from the hot sauce." Lilly grimaced before smiling sweetly, "Any questions?"

Matt ran through the list…"Spoke to Jessica, Thomas party, no lettuce wraps. Got it."

"Great," Lilly piped. "And also, tell Neil not to take the highway. Apparently there was some awful accident and traffic is totally backed up."

Magdalene and Matt nodded to Lilly and then left through the garage where Neil was waiting. As soon as they left I glanced with an amused expression at Lilly.

"It's a little ironic, don't you think? That Matt was just telling us how he *wouldn't* pose as a couple with Magdalene and now he's doing exactly that, but in order to get back at Grace."

33. Playing Dress Up

Matt and Magdalene walked up to the front desk of Ling's Cultural Chinese Bistro to be seated at their table.

"Hello, welcome to "Ling's Cultural Chinese Bistro," do you have a reservation?" a petite Chinese woman asked them snootily.

"Of course we do," Magdalene responded politely, "we spoke to Jessica over the phone and she reserved us a table on the balcony."

"Party name?" the woman asked drily.

"Thomas," Matt answered her bringing attention to himself for the first time.

The woman's jaw dropped, "Wait," she pointed out, utterly astonished, "You're Matt Martin! I love your show! And you," she gestured to Magdalene, "you're Magdalene Jule! I saw your debut on Broadway last summer! I was in one of the company boxes!"

Magdalene smiled sweetly, but said with a hint of irritation in her voice, "Really? That's wonderful. Now would you mind getting us to our table? We're famished."

"No, not at all," the woman said courteously, "Right this way. Oh and if anything isn't to your liking, my name is Ji Li."

"Thank you, Ji Li." Matt winked and grinned at her, making Ji Li blush. "Now if you wouldn't mind..." he looked at Magdalene suggestively as if they needed to be alone, on the inside he was complimenting himself on his acting skills. Who knew he would be so good at pretending he loved someone he really didn't? Well, actually, he had always known that...

Ji Li nodded furiously, "Not at all! Have a nice night." Ji Li wished them as she walked away hastily, her Jimmy Choo knock-offs clacking against the bamboo flooring.

"Now," Matt said to Magdalene as soon as she had walked away, "Grace is over there," he nodded over his left shoulder and Magdalene followed his glance.

"So, now what do we do?" Magdalene reached over and briefly touched his hand.

Matt caught on quickly, "Is she watching?"

Magdalene smiled at him from under her eyelashes, "You bet she is."

The two continued putting on a show while Grace not-so-slyly stole jealous glances in their (well mainly Magdalene's) direction and threw angry looks at Matt. At one point, Matt even caught her scornfully pointing over to them for her friend to see, who predictably, was also frowning in their direction.

"She looks peeved," Magdalene remarked to Matt when she looked over to see Grace raising a cynical eyebrow at the two of them, "I don't think she's too into you right now."

"Then the plan's working," Matt replied gleefully as he reached across the table to brush a strand of hair out of her face making Magdalene blush, "You know," Matt pointed out in an amused tone, "this is all fake, right?"

Magdalene scowled, "Yes," she snapped, "Of course, I do."

"Good," Matt smirked before adding, "And, may I add, people who are supposed to be in love don't glower at one another like you're doing right now."

Magdalene wiped away her scowl quickly and replied sulkily, "Sorry."

"Now," Matt went on, flagging over the waitress, "What would you like to drink, Maggy?"

Magdalene frowned at him, "It's *Magdalene*," she corrected him firmly.

"It was *supposed* to be a term of *endearment*, sweetie." Matt assured her forcing what he hoped did not look like a strained smile.

Magdalene ignored him and turned to the nervous waitress, "We'd like two iced waters with lemon."

♥♥♥

"Wait," Lilly interrupted Magdalene who had been recalling their first date later that night, "Why don't you like being called Maggy? It's such an adorable name!"

Magdalene rolled her eyes, "Exactly. I don't want to be considered *adorable*," she spat out the word like it was poison. "I want to be a character actor not an ingénue. And, my publicist fears that being adorable and cute would get in the way of that."

Without thinking, I snorted, "Well, that's stupid."

Magdalene shot me an icy cold glare and said snootily, "I'll have you know that my publicist is the top in the business. She is the *god* of publicists. Besides, what would you know? You're just a high school student."

I beg her pardon?

"Excuse me, but, it isn't like you're so old or mature either. I mean, you're only 18!"

"That," she smugly pointed out, "is considered an *adult*."

Oh, my shoulders slumped, she had a point there.

"Well," Matt clapped his hands nervously, "I, personally, am ready to get back to that wonderful story about our evening so how about I take it from here."

"Actually," Magdalene dithered, "I think I'll head home before anything or *someone*," she glimpsed in my direction pointedly, "gets out of hand."

My eyebrows shot up, "Yeah, we wouldn't want *that* would we?"

"Come on you two, let's not let an itty bitty argument get in the way of our fun," Lilly piped in; I shot her a quick, irritated look. "Or not," Lilly pitifully mumbled in a tiny voice.

Magdalene stood up and grabbed her purse, "Lilly, you need a ride home?"

Yes, I waited for her to answer. We had almost run out of gas on the ride back from Sephora. She only had seven miles worth left of gas.

"Nope," Lilly smiled proudly, "I have a car now, I turned 16 a few days ago." Lilly paused, frowning, "Well, actually, I don't really have a car. Or not a very good car...it's kind of dumpy. I mean, the gray exterior is dull, the interior looks a bit cheap because…it's made of like, *carpet*. Am I the only one who thinks that's a little odd, carpet interior?" Lilly looked as us expectantly.

I looked at Lilly blankly. Matt looked at her blankly, even Magdalene had stopped in her tracks.

Lilly sighed, feeling sorry for herself, "My car *sucks*. Doesn't it? Why couldn't I have gotten a cute little Beemer that I could hang plush dice from the rearview mirror?" Lilly sighed again loudly and snatched her keys from the kitchen table where we were holding court, "Well," she moped, giving us a tiny, half-hearted wave, "I guess I'll be seeing ya."

Lilly walked out the door with her head ducked and Magdalene cooed earnestly, "Aw that was so sad."

I rolled my eyes in belittlement, "Come on," I scoffed, "it's a car, not the Armageddon. She'll survive, she always does. She survived her hair, she'll survive this."

Magdalene frowned in befuddlement, "Why? What happened to her hair?"

Matt chuckled to himself, "The hairstylist made a horrible mistake and dyed it."

"And cut it short." I reminded him.

"And cut it short," Matt added, "what a sob story," he ended sarcastically.

"What color did it used to---," Magdalene began before Lilly came back bursting through the double doors.

"Hey, Magdalene," she interrupted meekly, "I don't know when it happened, but I ran out of gas. I might need that ride home..."

34. More Causes, More Effects

"Lilly," I tried to reason, "I don't see why, or *how*, you did this."

Lilly rolled her eyes, "I see why I did this perfectly and it was easy to accomplish since Daddy owns the luxury car dealership I bought it at. All the staff just assumed he knew what I was up to," she said staring at her shiny new Beemer proudly. "And besides, after I traded the old one in it only cost, like, twenty five thousand dollars." Lilly shrugged carelessly, "And, if daddy gets pissed, who cares? He still owes me my thirteenth birthday present and a Christmas present from last year."

I knit my eyebrows together, not seeing how this would add up.

Lilly saw my concerned expression and laughed, "Carrie, lighten up, will you? I've got a cool new car to drag you around in! You should be happy!"

"I *am* happy," I assured her, making her grin smugly, "that," I added, "I'm not going to be the one getting the hammer later on when your dad finds out about...*this*!" I made wild gestures at her new cream colored convertible.

Lilly waved a hand at me, brushing my comments aside, "Whatever, Carrie. You thought the same thing when I bought myself that silver Cartier bracelet."

"You used your *dad's* credit card!" I practically shouted at her, "Without even asking!"

"Whatever," Lilly sighed like I was pointless. "So," her face brightened and she clapped her hands, "Matt is aware his next date is tomorrow for lunch at Dewey's Vineyard Salad Bar, yes?"

I nodded and said in a corny cheery tone, "He's dreading it."

Without hearing me, Lilly went on, "Excellent! Now, I made reservations with Casey Caster at..."

Lilly drones on, but I'm barely listening, instead I'm looking over her shoulder at one of the gardeners working on the Thomas' rose bushes. Something was wrong about the way his canvas vest fell over his damp shirt, it was almost as if...

"Shh!" I whispered trying to silence Lilly's endless chatter.

"What? Why?" Lilly pouted her freshly glossed lips, "Listen, if this is about my car, I get it, I know you don't support me being so..."

"Irresponsible?" I finished her sentence, than shook my head trying to remain focused, "Lilly, I need you to go inside."

Lilly cocks her head curiously, "Why?"

"To…" To what? I look back to the gardener, I can still see the camera and recorder imprint through his sheer, thin shirt. I needed to shut Lilly up about the dating stuff. However, since she wasn't letting on how the whole thing was a sham and hadn't even mentioned that the girl Matt was dating was Magdalene, it isn't like any real harm could be done.

But still, what if Lilly accidentally slips up and reveals these major details? What if Matt doesn't want word getting out about his supposed romance with Magdalene? What if he wants his revenge to be more private?

"What do you need, Carrie?" asked Lilly.

"Um…I need a glass of water," I blurted.

Lilly squinted her eyes at me questioningly, but began to walk inside. I sighed with relief, for once my blabber mouth friend would not be starting any gossip. I was just pivoting around to face the "gardener" triumphantly and tell him how today wasn't going to be his lucky day when Lilly briefly turned around and called back:

"I'm so excited about our plan, Carrie! I can't believe Matt's really going to go through with this whole dating Magdalene thing! I think this could really work out!"

Oopsie!

35. Word Gets Out

Two days later, after Matt has had a successful sham date with Magdalene, the mailman delivers my weekly *Gilbertson Gossip* with this headline:

Exclusively from G. Gossip:

Matt Martin and Magdalene Jule Are Just Heating Up!

- According to a close family friend "I think this relationship could really work out!" and "Matt's really going to go through with this [relationship with Jule]!"

- Martin and Jule have already been spotted on steamy, romantic dates!

I stare down at the headline and its slightly altered quotes. Above it are two separate pictures: one of Matt playing Daniel on *Ignorance is Bliss* and one Magdalene on Broadway.

"Hey Matt," I call tentatively, "Have you by chance seen the cover of this week's issue *Gilbertson Gossip* yet?"

Matt comes down the stairs wearing basketball shorts and an Under Armor shirt with some Nike running shoes, "Um, no, I haven't, but can it wait? I'm scheduled to go running with Magdalene today. We're going to run by Grace's condo when she should be leaving for work." Matt smirked, "This plan of Lilly's is dynamite. I didn't think it would really work, but Grace seemed really provoked at Dewey's yesterday."

I rush him along, "Yeah, yeah, that's all fine and dandy Matt, but can I just show you the magazine super quick? It'll only take five seconds," I plead, making prayer hands in front of my face and batting big puppy dog eyes.

"Fine," Matt conceded, "Show me."

I show him the cover.

"Who," Matt inquires, "is this 'close family friend' they are referring to?"

"Lilly." I respond in a small voice, "They overheard us talking, I tried to stop her once I spotted the photographer who was dressed as a gardener, but she slipped about Magdalene right before she walked inside. Those quotes though, they are totally altered, she did not say that," I bit my lower lip, "Well, actually, she basically did...but, she didn't say that *exactly*!"

Matt shrugged, "'I'll go over this with Magdalene, see what she wants to do, and then I'll ask Rebecca to make a statement either way."

I was impressed by how calmly Matt was handling this. Normally he was such a drama queen, or rather king.

"Now," Matt declared resolutely, "I am going to go for my run with Magdalene."

An hour after Matt left I received a text from Lilly.

LILLY'S MOBILE: OMG!!!! did u c g.gossip? I am SO sorry. ☹

MY MOBILE: yes, I know...no worries, Matt has it covered.

LILLY'S MOBILE: ok thx ☺ well hope it all goes well ☺

I'm about to reply when I get a text from some random number.

5558870763: I saw the headline.

I frown, who is this? I feel like I'm in some thriller about a creepy, unidentified stalker.

MY MOBILE: who is this???

5558870763: grace

MY MOBILE: okidokie then, hello grace.

5558870763: do u really not know who this is?? ur brother's ex gf...works 4 Cole Collins...the girl whose life ur trying 2 ruin?

MY MOBILE: I am not trying 2 ruin ur life grace

5558870763: right...so why then r u & ur friends setting up some lame ploy 2 make me jealous by making me always see matt and magdalene on dates?

MY MOBILE: wow, for a cheater u catch on quick

5558870763: ha. ha. whatever. having matt date a girl he obviously is not into & making them run by my house when matt told me he hates jogging is a pretty dumb way of getting revenge

MY MOBILE: idk grace...u seemed a little peeved at their last date.

5558870763: and u wouldn't b?

MY MOBILE: fine. whatever. see ur point.

5558870763: well, love 2 stay & chat but i have a date 2 go on ☺

5558870763: and don't bother coming.

MY MOBILE: ha. ha. who is the date with?

5558870763: matt martin ☺

Apparently, I'm not the only one with a few tricks up her sleeve.

Part Five

Grace (x2)

36. Foggy Notions

"What do you think she meant, by having a date with Matt, I mean?" I twirl my old fashioned phone's cord around my ankle.

"Well," Lilly's sounded pitchy and juvenile over the phone. "Apparently Grace intends on getting Matt back."

I scratched the back of my neck in thought, "I guess that could make sense. It just seemed like such a spur of the moment comment! I wonder if she just wanted to mess with my head."

Lilly clucked her tongue, "I don't see why you're so pessimistic about all this. After all, it's all so romantic! Wouldn't you just die if this happened to you?" Lilly sighed dreamily.

"Yeah," I sardonically replied, "of stress."

"You're so...*rational* these days! What happened to girl who only wanted to help her brother find true love?" Lilly asked sadly, "She was more fun to talk to."

"I still want that for Matt and I'm not saying I don't want to have a thrilling romance someday..." I left my sentence unfinished and stared out my window absentmindedly.

"Carolyn? Are you still there?" Lilly brought me back to Earth.

I shook my head trying to wake myself up. I hadn't gotten any sleep last night since I couldn't stop dwelling over Grace's text. Every time I would try to close my eyes and go to sleep I would find myself tossing and turning trying to figure it out, like an impossible geometry problem.

"I'm sorry, Lilly; I'm just a little...beleaguered that's all." I try to assure my fairytale loving friend.

"Ok," she sounds unconvinced, "if you say so. Listen, I'm sorry, but I have to go. Pilates."

I sigh. "Have fun," I tell her idly.

"I will," Lilly laughs, "Now, try to take a nap, Carrie. You sound exhausted."

Click. Lilly hangs up the phone and I untangle my ankle from the phone cord. It is covered in pink spiral imprints. I collapse back on my beanbag chair and do exactly that, take a nap.

♥♥♥

In my dreams Matt is a knight. In fact, he's a knight in shining armor embellished with sapphires and white gold swirls. He's fighting a meek, timid looking dragon with a shaggy blonde hairdo quite similar to his own and with the same piercing blue eyes. In between them both is Grace.

I've heard that at any given moment Shakespeare's sonnets and plays will tell you exactly what you need to know, but I think the same goes with dreams. Even if they make no freaking sense—like hiking might to a devoted video game junkie.

"Matty," I barge into his room and yank open the drapes making him groan, "You need to ask Grace out."

"Why? I thought you hated her just like me." Matt's voice comes out muffled from under his pillows.

"Well," I say smugly, "I had quite the enlightenment during my nap today, yes I did take a nap today and I don't care how babyish it sounds because you are taking a nap too---,"

Matt breaks me off, "*Was* taking a nap." Matt corrects me, "Past tense."

I huff, "Sorry, you *were* taking a nap too. Anyway, I had an interesting dream."

"Is there a point to this monologue?" Matt remarks harshly still buried in a sea of pillows.

I put my hands on my hips, "Do you want to hear this story or not?"

"Fine, go on."

I explain my dream to Matt only to get a blank look in return, "I don't get it."

Frustrated by his lack of quixotic vision, I throw my head into my hands and say, "Don't you see, Matt? You're fighting against yourself here! You're trying to convince yourself you don't still have feelings for Grace—that you don't still love her! You want to go out with her, but you simply won't permit yourself!" I wave my arms around dramatically, "It's so wasteful! To push her away like that when all you want to do is pull her back in!" I sigh and fall on to the foot of his bed.

Matt comes out from under his pillows, his blonde hair a tangled nest, he gives me a quizzical glance, "So, you think I am pushing Grace away from me and that I should just put it all out there and go ahead and ask her out?"

I nod animatedly.

"But, what if she says no?" Matt asks downheartedly.

"She won't say no." I promise him, "In fact, I have proof." I stand up and begin skipping out of the room enthusiastically and exclaim back as I go, "GRACE SOMEHOW GOT MY NUMBER, YOU SEE, AND SHE SENT ME THESE BIZARRE TEXTS ABOUT HOW SHE SAW THE HEADLINE AND KNOWS ABOUT OUR, QUOTE ON

QUOTE: 'LAME PLOY TO GET REVENGE' AND HOW SHE KNOWS YOU HATE JOGGING." I fumble through my drawers looking for my phone, "ANYWAYS, SHE APPARENTLY WASN'T THAT IMPRESSED. ALTHOUGH, SHE DID ADMIT SHE WAS STILL A BIT," I reenter Matt's room, practically panting, "put out by our scam." Matt grinned haughtily at this, "So then she said she had to go because she had a date and guess who she said it was with?"

I shove my phone under Matt's nose.

37. Dozens of Roses

Turns out, I was right, about Grace wanting Matt back and him secretly yearning for her. When Matt called her and asked her to come to his costar's Leo Urban's annual August 1st "Bliss for Australia" party a fundraiser for preserving the Barrier Reef and its wildlife, she literally jumped at the opportunity to reunite with Matt and mend their relationship.

"I told you she still liked you," I boasted arrogantly and I straightened Matt's Hugo Boss tie, "You know, I could be a psychic since I'm so good at predicting things. I bet I would never be wrong," I added jokingly as I brushed some lint off of Matt's tan sports jacket.

Although you might think the party would be all laid back and relaxed it was actually pretty formal. Leo referred to the dress code as "Summer Fancy" which meant guys should wear a sports jacket and tie and girls should wear cocktail dresses. I wonder what Grace will wear...

Matt smiled, but changed the topic, "So, when are you even going to get dressed?"

I puckered my brow in confusion, "Since when am I coming?"

"Uh," Matt pretended to stroke his chin, "since now."

I freak out, "WHY DIDN'T YOU TELL ME EARLIER? I DON'T EVEN KNOW WHAT I'M GOING TO WEAR!" I smack his shoulder playfully, "*You* can get ready by yourself!"

Crap. Seriously, why didn't he run this by me? I have no idea what to wear! Sure, Alexa let me keep that Valentino from the premiere, but I don't want to wear that. I do have the Vera Wang Lavender Label from the Make-A-Wish thing, but I forgot to get it dry cleaned afterwards.

I search frantically around my closet. I find an organza George Chakra Couture mini that had had a train until my mom insisted we took it off. That could work, I try it on and revel at how the pink and gray colors play up my auburn hair. This is definitely what I'll wear. I begin to parade into the hallway, in love with my decision.

I step carefully down the stair and I'm almost halfway down when my mom comes out of the den and sees me. A wide smile breaks across her face.

"Do you like it?" I ask her, doing a little twirl.

"You look beautiful, honey!" my mom gushes making me blush, "But, weren't you going to have it altered a little in the," she hushes her voice to a whisper, "*chest area* so it isn't as gappy?"

I bend over and sure enough, there is a perfect view of my bra. Damn it. I walk back up the stairs with my shoulders slumped.

I slip out of the dress and hang it on my door. I do some more searching, all the while shivering in my bra and panties, but too lazy to put on a shirt. Finally I find a cute (but casual) Lipsy floral dress. After some hesitation I slip it on and play it up with some jewelry and bright blue Prada heels. I smile. It'll do. I could always put up my hair in a cute, sloppy bun or something…

I traipse down the stairs and do another spin for my mom who was waiting. She tsks me:

"Carolyn, sweetie, don't be silly, it is much too casual!"

"But…" I begin; nothing irritates me more when my mom doesn't trust my outfit judgment. Besides, it's not like I even *asked* for her opinion.

"But, nothing, sweetie," my mom raises her eyebrows disapprovingly.

"Fine," I grumble, marching back into my room.

I ended up deciding on a very light gray ruffled silk chiffon and leather Hermes skirt that reaches about mid thigh and a silk light blue tank. Despite my mom's arguments I paired them with patent leather Jimmy Choo wedges. Take that Mom.

Matt and Grace, who had came over in a short black strapless Moschino with a tightly wrapped upper half that flowed into a bouncy skirt, had abandoned me to go to the party. So I had to be driven by *my parents* to a big time celebrity (it makes no difference that I interact with celebrities on a daily basis) party! I mean, come on! Cameron Diaz is going to be there! I don't want to be driven by my parents to a party with the likes of Cameron Diaz!

I get out of the car as quickly and soon as possible without giving them a second glance. Luckily, I don't think anyone saw me exit, except for, of course, Ashton Kutcher.

After giving him a shy wave I storm off to find Matt and Grace, my *abandoners.* I spotted them instantly, nestled close together by the bar.

"*Excuuuuuse* me," I sneak up on them using as masculine of a voice I can muster, "but aren't you two underage?"

Both Matt and Grace whirl around on their stools with wide, mortified eyes, but once they see me they both erupt in laughter, making me feel like a joke. Matt tries to stop laughing, but his remark comes out with guffaws mixed in between words:

"What were you going to do," he glimpses at Grace with an entertained smirk, "arrest us?"

I crossed my arms and raised my eyebrows, trying to sound more stern than I felt, "I could certainly tell Mom and Dad and I'm certain they wouldn't have a problem dealing with you."

Matt rolls his eyes and hands his white wine to a passing waiter in a tuxedo along with Grace's martini, "Point taken."

I smile triumphantly, "Oh, and thanks for leaving me stuck at home, by the way, I can tell how important I am to both of you." I snap condescendingly, "I was only the one who repaired you're beloved relationship."

"We're sorry," Matt reassures me, although Grace doesn't look it.

"Thank you," I chirp happily. "Now, I'll leave you both to your cuddling, but try not to get drunk, ok?" I implore, always the voice of reason.

Grace smiles, "We'll try." Then she turns back to Matt and pulls him into a big kiss.

After the party I was lying on the couch reading. I heard a door creak open and I looked up to see Matt, or rather, a slightly unsteady Matt.

"Hi there," I greet him, patting the cushion next to me, "Have anything else to drink tonight?"

As Matt makes his way over, he sways only a tad on one step.

"Uh..." he thinks it over, "Nope." He smiles widely, "Aren't you proud of me?"

Hesitantly, I pat his knee, "Of course, I am," I smile back, feeling like a mom.

"I really like Gracie," Matt sighs as he burrows into the couch cushions, "I *love* her, Carrie. She's pretty and sweet and pretty and...sweet. I," Matt sighs again and looks at the ceiling contentedly, "love her!"

I grin, but tilt my head quizzically at him. When he says nothing I ask him to wait a second and I run up stairs to get my (untouched for almost a month!) notebook so I can add some stuff about Grace.

When I bring it back down, Matt gazes at it for awhile before asking, "What's that, a *diiiiiiary*?"

I chuckle and reply, "No, it's a...research project."

Matt knits his eyebrows together, "Over the summer?"

"Sure," I answer only to look up and see he's fallen asleep. He almost looks angelic with a small little smile and his knees bent up practically to his chin.

I open the notebook and read what I have so far, crossing out everything as I go.

~~Libby:~~

- ~~has already dated Matt...evident they have good chemistry~~
- ~~PRETTY~~
- ~~fun to be around~~
- ~~intelligent~~
- ~~loves Matt's guts~~ ☺
- ~~Reasons why she shouldn't be Matt's "princess": can be clingy, hard to please at times, a little over 3 year age difference, their relationship already failed once, and not to mention it is ILLEGAL for Matt to be dating a minor~~

~~Alexa:~~

- ~~"good kisser"~~
- ~~PRETTY!!~~
- ~~Matt still likes her~~

- ~~successful, smart~~

~~Reasons why she shouldn't be Matt's "princess": she's still is furious~~
~~with Matt, is it a problem they work together?, their relationship~~
~~already failed once~~ ☹

Grace:

- has a laid back vibe that Matt finds sexy
- as if by fate, she too ordered a pumpkin spice latte this morning
- "pretty and sweet and pretty and sweet..."
- Matt is completely and undyingly (no exaggeration) in love with her

Obviously, there isn't anyone else for Matt. For him to admit (more than once) that he loves her and go on about what he likes about her to me (at a time other than if he's lecturing me about breaking him and someone up), it must mean that he's committed. And not just, I-won't-cheat-on-you committed, but through thick and thin, bad and good, he'd always be there for her. Awww.

38. Three Way Phone Calls

Fine, I'm guilty, I'm listening in on another one of Matt and Grace's lovey-dovey phone calls.

It's been a month since Leo Urban's party (summer is almost over!) and Matt and Grace have been completely *inseparable* since. They have had a romantic outing every day (ranging from picnics on the beach, a trip to Yosemite, camping out in our front room watching movies, or going out to eat) and usually have a long and conversation packed phone call every day.

"*Soooo*," Grace drawled. "What are we going to do tomorrow?"

Matt clears his throat and apologetically admits, "About that...I can't go out tomorrow. I have to go meet someone..."

Probably some boring meeting with Rebecca and Tony or maybe it's another thing about his Cole Collins' movie.

"Oh? Who?" Grace sounds neglected and sad.

"Oh, just a family member of a friend; don't worry, I won't be having any fun either." Matt laughs stiffly trying to comfort her.

Grace laughs quietly before persisting on her quest for answers, "Why? Would I know them?"

"Well, it's a close friend's of dad; he's going to help me with a big decision I have to make. You...you probably know them," Matt answers, obviously choosing his words carefully.

Now, who is this "close friend's of dad" and what is this "big decision"? It could be Rebecca's dad, the founder of Mishker Productions. Maybe it has to do with the movie?

It could also be our half cousins', Nina and Mark's, dad, Uncle Rick, who is, like, the COO of some major bank. Maybe Matt's going to open an important account?

Grace begins talking and I snap back to attention, "Oh. Well, want to do something for dinner? Surely it won't take all day."

"I think we should just wait until Friday. I don't want to risk my meeting running later than expected and you be stuck waiting," says Matt earnestly.

"Oh ok, but I can't do Friday, Mr. Collins is having me run through the cast once more and then make sure everyone has an assistant. He's also having me call Jewel to confirm she'll do some songs for the movie. It doesn't sound like it would take all day, but this normally takes me hours."

"Well, how about lunch on Saturday then?" Matt suggests, "I might have...something to do that morning, some errands to run, but I'll be able to do lunch."

"That works!" Grace replies joyfully, "Oh, damn. Look at the time!"

Without thinking, I check the time; it's almost 10:05 p.m.! I've been listening to their phone call for over an hour and a half. I find that their phone calls are an amazing way to pass the time, like a good book.

"I have to go," Grace apologizes gloomily; "Got to get some beauty sleep!" she laughs at herself.

"You're so beautiful, Grace, that you don't even need beauty sleep."

My heart is still melting as they say their goodbyes and hang up the phone. The whole night I dream about a boy saying that to me someday.

39. Road Trip

"Matty, where are you off to this beautiful morning?" I ask Matt with honest curiosity as I pour myself a bowl of peanut butter Captain Crunch without milk.

"I have to meet someone," He says vaguely as he devours his Lucky Charms (with milk) that I can remember him having for breakfast since we were little.

"Do you want to talk to me about it?"

"About what?" questions Matt, gazing up from his cereal with a drop of milk dripping down his chin.

I pretend to wipe my chin as a signal to Matt and he wipes his chin too, "Obviously you have something you're going to be talking to this person about. I was wondering if I could know what it is."

"I'd rather not tell you yet because I'm not sure if it will even happen, but, trust me, you will be the first to know if all works out." He gobbles down the rest of his cereal and washes the dish before leaving to change.

"Must be pretty important," I comment to Matt when he comes down the stairs in khakis and a white linen button down.

"You could say that."

40. A Father's Blessing

When Matt comes to the dinner table that
evening, still dressed in his khakis and button down, he
looks enthralled, nervous, and radiant at the same time.
As he sits down he gives me a meaningful look.

"I like your shirt, honey," Mom tells Matt.

Matt takes a big bite of pasta, "Thanks."

"Mouth closed," Dad barks quickly.

"So, how was your meeting today?" I ask Matt,
sparking curious expressions on our parents' faces.

"It was good," he beamed, "I met Grace's dad."

Our dad pats him on the back, "That's my boy,
always a gentleman."

"And...um..." Matt glimpses at me nervously,
"I...I asked him for Grace's hand in marriage."

41. Disapproval

I nearly choke.

I can't believe he would do that.

He's going to marry Grace.

He is seriously going to *marry* her.

Why would he be so happy if Grace's father had said no?

♥♥♥

"Are you out of your mind?" I cry, "You are going to get married?!"

Matt frightened expression tells me all I need to know.

My mom is on the edge of hysterics, "But, honey, you're so *young.*"

"Matt," my dad scolds him sternly, "I'm afraid I will not allow you to get married. You didn't even ask your own parents first. We won't let you throw your life away like that."

Matt scowls and snaps, "But, I wasn't even asking for your opinion! Truth of the matter is, it's done.

I'm buying the ring Saturday and then I'm proposing. I don't care, what you think! I love her, Dad, and I'm going to spend the rest of my life with her."

Mom tears up, "But, she hasn't even said yes."

42. Bystander

I agree with my parents.

This all seems a little rash.

I don't want Matt to screw up.

Sure, it's romantic, but...

It *is* really sweet...

"I support Matt," I say quietly.

No one hears me.

Is that a sign?

Should I shut up?

"Matt," my dad is saying, "You are not getting married."

"Dad, I'll do what I want," Matt shouts back, "Can't you just try, for once in your life, trusting me?"

My dad's face is turning red, "This is a little different than doing a sitcom or an Oprah interview, Matt, and this is your *life* we're talking about here!"

♥♥♥

How did things get so chaotic?

Can't they just try and trust him?

As Mom said, she hasn't even said yes yet.

At least let him ask.

♥♥♥

My dad is full on yelling now, "How could you have been so inconsiderate of your mother?" he glances over at Mom who is weeping softly, "How could you be so selfish?"

"I'm not trying to be!" Matt yells back, "I was just trying to share some news with my family when you began gnashing your teeth!"

I rub my temples.

Dad doesn't even realize he's making Mom more upset than Matt is.

No mother likes seeing a father and son fight.

"Carolyn, are you even going to try to help me out here?" Matt whispers to me frantically.

My parents stare at me, "You knew about this, Carolyn?" my mom asks softly.

I bite my lower lip and reply in a small voice, "No, not exactly..."

"Good." Dad says firmly, "Now go up to your room or go to a friend's if you'd like. Your mother and I have to talk for a little while with Matt."

43. Rule Breakers

All of this yelling is annoying.

Matt's, in particular.

I was no help at all.

But, what was I supposed to do?

Lie that I knew all about Matt's plans?

Scream to the world how much I agree with Matt?

Especially when I'm not even sure if I do?

♥♥♥

Finally, right when I swore my head was going to explode, the yelling ceases. Matt walks straight into my room and remarks glumly:

"Thanks, you were a big help out there."

I let his sour comment pass and say, "So you really asked her dad if you could marry her?"

"Yep."

I whistle softly, "You must be pretty serious about her."

Matt looks up and rolls his eyes at me, "Really? I hadn't figured that out yet."

Embarrassed, I stare at the floor, "I was just saying."

Matt makes a face at me, "Whatever."

"So, you never told me how the fight ended you know." I glance at him apprehensively.

"I'm not allowed to marry her," he pauses.

I pat his back awkwardly, "I'm sorry, Matty. It was a really sweet idea. I thought it was kind of a charming notion, such a young, impromptu marriage like that. Like something out of a poem."

Matt breaks into a mischievous smile, "That is exactly why I'm still going to ask her."

44. Wedding Plans

I call Grace the next morning posing as a survey conductor. I know, lame, right? But, it's the only way I'll be able to get an honest answer.

"Hello?"

"Hi this is Halle Berger from---," I begin.

"This is Grace. Sorry I'm not able to answer the phone right now, so leave a message after the beep and I'll try to get back to you as soon as I can! Bye!"

"Damn," I mutter, slamming down the phone, Matt looks over at me from his perch in front of my computer where he's been looking through jewelers' websites.

"Voicemail?" Matt asks knowingly without even removing his gaze from the computer screen.

"Of course."

Matt pauses, "Try her home phone."

"Wow, that'd be a great idea if I actually knew the number," I retort.

"It's 555...658...0902." Matt recites dryly.

I dial the number, as it rings, I remark to Matt, "You have it *memorized*?"

Matt catches himself and blushes, "Maybe..."

I laugh and a regal voice picks up the phone, "Hello? This is Jolene."

Alarmed I cover the receiver and murmur to Matt, "I think it's her mom! Who should I pretend to be?"

"Be a person from work!"

I uncover the phone, "Hello, Jolene. This is...Martha Stewart," Matt snickers and I throw a pillow at him.

"*Oof!*" Matt grunts.

"Um...Ms. Stewart? Are you still there?" Jolene speculates.

"Oh yes, I'm sorry, the phone reception is horrible here."

"And, where are you exactly?"

"California," I reply, "I'm actually a coworker of Grace and I was wondering if I could speak to her?" I ask professionally.

"Yes, wait one second." Jolene pulls away from the phone, "Grace!" she calls, "Martha...Stewart's on the phone for you!"

Grace picks up the phone, "Hello?"

"Hi Grace, this is Martha, you might remember me from work," *Not.* "I'm part of a survey group so I was calling requesting an answer to the question." I pause as if I'm reading the question, "What is your favorite precious metal?"

"I like sterling silver," Grace responds unsurely.

"Thank you! That'll be all!" I say abruptly, hanging up the phone.

"So," Matt concludes, "what is it then?"

"Sterling silver," I report.

"That's perfect! I know the perfect place for us to look!"

"Us?" I ask him, surprised.

"Well, I'm going to need a girl's opinion and you, my loving sister, are indeed a girl."

"I feel like we've gone over this before."

Matt chuckles, "And, we will again."

45. Breakfast at Tiffany's

As we drive up to Tiffany & Co. in Matt's black BMW 650i I fire at him with questions:

"Do you have any idea what you want it to look like?"

"Nope."

"Are you going to want any different gemstones asides from diamonds?"

"Not sure."

"Maybe you could have something engraved inside the ring?" I suggest.

Matt shrugs, "Maybe."

"Do you want an indoor or outdoor wedding?"

"We'll cross that bridge when we get to it."

I ask in astonishment, "Do you have anything planned?"

"Aside from proposing to her?" Matt glimpses at me, "No."

I sit back and exhale loudly, "For being so set on getting married you sure don't have any ideas about the actual details."

Matt shrugs, "Why should I? I'm going to hire a wedding planner."

I stare at him in shock, "That's so *insensitive*! You're going to hire some overpriced, old lady who probably has never been married to plan your wedding for you?!"

"Whoa, whoa, whoa, Carolyn, calm down. If Grace would rather not hire a wedding planner, we won't."

"Good," I nod my head in agreement.

The two of us walk into Tiffany's, passing by a familiar looking lanky redhead who is, not so slyly, sneaking peeks at Matt every ten seconds as we pick out a ring.

A lady with a whimsical air and large, dangly earrings behind the counter comes up to us and asks, "Can I help you with anything today?"

"Um, sure, we're trying to find an engagement ring," Matt answers her nervously.

The lady clasps her hands and smiles warmly at us. "Aw, young love! Excuse my asking, but when are you two tying the knot? I love weddings."

I widen my eyes and throw up my hands, "I'm sorry, but you've made a mistake. We're," I switch my hands back and forth between Matt and I, "*not* getting married."

The lady's face falls flat and she comments dryly, "Then, why are *you* here?"

"I'm his sister, Carolyn. Hi." I reach out to shake her hand as I've seen my mom do in jewelry stores so many times before, but the lady takes no notice of my gesture so I pull it back awkwardly and pretend to scratch the back of my neck.

"But, you are still going to get married, yes?" she snubs me turning to Matt who does a little nod.

"And, are you looking for anything special?" she persists.

I nudge Matt and he opens his mouth, "Um..."

Obviously, Matt here isn't going to be the one taking charge. I wouldn't be surprised if I'm the one who ends up proposing to Grace.

"He's looking for a ring made with sterling silver perhaps something we could have a message engraved inside?"

"Very well." The lady leads us to a display case next to a floor to ceiling window where you can view the insane traffic outside. "These are a few choices, but I suggest narrowing it down to a certain style," she pauses and adds, "I am partial to the more classical style as opposed to something more modern and angular."

"Classical sounds good," Matt lets the lady know.

"Wonderful," she pushes away all the rings that could be classified as modern and continues, holding up a sparkly ring, "I am not sure if you would be for this arrangement, but this three row ring with the teardrop shape diamonds is at its height right now."

I turn to Matt, "That's nice. Do you like that?"

"What else is there?"

The lady pushes aside the ring and brings up another, this time it's more simple with just four dainty diamonds, "This would probably be considered the opposite of the last one...it's effortless and would never go out of style."

"Too plain," Matt stops for a second, "She's not a nun or a feminist."

"Excuse my," I shoot Matt a pointed glare, "ill-mannered brother. He's very tense today."

"No I'm not!" Matt counters.

"Yes," I say through gritted teeth, "you are."

Matt scowls, but stays silent.

After showing us seven more rings the lady throws up her hands, "Ok, I'm sorry, but obviously he has something in mind. So how about I let you two browse on your own."

I smile at sweetly, "That'd be lovely."

As soon as she walks away Matt throws a scoffing glance my way, "*Lovely*?"

I glare at him, "You know what? It was the first thing to cross my mind and I've needed to make up for your lack of manners!"

"Whatever," he glowers, "Let's just pick a ring and be done with it...how about that one?" he points to matte finished gold ring that forms a heart around a single clear diamond.

"It's pretty," I admit, "but I think it's more of a promise ring."

"What's the difference? *Promise...engagement...* same thing!"

"Actually, they're not," I inform him, "A promise ring is when---,"

Matt cuts me off, "I don't care. That is the ring I want and that is what I am going to get. She'll love it."

"If you're absolutely positive..."

"Carolyn, don't worry, I'm positive." Matt persuades me.

♥♥♥

"Have you found everything you need today?" the man who is ringing up Matt's purchase asks us.

"Yes, we have," Matt responds cheerfully.

The man places the ring in a classic baby blue Tiffany's box and ties a delicate ribbon around it. When he's finished he smiles and hands the box to Matt and then looks at me and says, "You are one lucky girl, miss."

I shake my head, "I'm not his *fiancée*. I'm his *sister*."

"My apologies," the guy responds to us before adding, pointing to the box, "But, you both are aware this is a *promise* ring not an *engagement* ring?"

Matt sighs and assures him irritably, "We are aware."

"Ok, good, now you both have a terrific afternoon!"

"You, too," I say as we make our way to leave. Once we're out of hearing distance I lean into Matt, "Why does everyone seem to think we're engaged?"

"Probably because, seeing you have none of my dashing looks, they don't realize we're actually related."

I punch him in the arm...just in time for the lanky redhead to take a picture of us on her camera phone.

46. The Big Question

I'm sorry to say this is not the first time I've spied on one of Matt and Grace's dates behind a bush. And I'm sorry to say it won't be my last.

Matt and I decided he would propose to Grace today at lunch. We stopped at a florist to buy a dozen pink roses (as opposed to the highly clichéd red). Then we drove by the house so Matt could change out of his distressed jeans and white t-shirt and drop me off. However, unbeknownst to him, I took Dad's "weekend car" without a license (I have a permit though...) and followed him. I'm sorry, but this is simply a date, I cannot miss.

"Hello Matty," Grace greets him, giving him a light kiss on the cheek sweetly.

"Hi," Matt replies softly.

"Something wrong?" concern fills Grace's voice.

"How is that possible when I get to go out with a gorgeous girl like you?" Matt comments charmingly.

"I honestly don't know." Grace shrugs and throws him a small, flirtatious smile.

Matt pulls out Grace's chair and orders some champagne (I'll scold him later) because "it's a special occasion" and after the waiter finishes staring at them disapprovingly, he actually brings it to them.

Grace tilts her head and grins coyly, "May I ask what the special occasion is?"

"Hmm...I don't know about that."

"Oh please tell me," Grace clasps her hand like she's praying, "I'll give you anything in return!"

Matt pretends to hesitate, clucking his tongue thoughtfully, "I'm still not convinced...it would probably depend on what you offer," he raises his eyebrows as if to say *bring it on*.

"Is that a challenge?"

"If you want it to be, sure, it's a challenge."

"How about a kiss?" Grace suggests.

"Isn't that pretty much required anyway?" he asks incredulously.

Grace laughs, shaking her head, "If you don't want a kiss what else could you possibly want?"

Matt gets up, taking the ring box from his pocket. Even though I know what's coming, I gasp. Grace gasps, too.

"Is that...?" she leaves her sentence suspended in the air like a balloon.

"Grace..." Matt kneels down on one knee, emitting a chorus of gasps from people sitting close by.

"Cynthia, look! That boy is proposing!" a young girl squeals.

"Omigosh! That is *soooo* sweet!" another girl gushes.

"Wait a moment, isn't that Matt Martin?" one lady asks.

"It is!" another responds, "but who's that girl? I've never seen her before!"

"He's proposing to her! That's all that matters!" the last lady silences her.

"Hey, that's the guy from *Ignorance is Bliss*! a man exclaims causing nearly every lady in the restaurant to hush him.

Grace, who was on the verge of tears, laughs and tries to joke, "They never stop watching you, do they?"

Matt smiles, but ignores her joke, "Grace, we've only known each other since almost the beginning of the summer and for, like, five days we weren't even dating..." he gives a weak laugh, "but the point is, it has been the best summer of my entire life. I love you so much Grace. You're beautiful, smart, funny, and all the things I've ever dreamed of. I talked to your dad and...Grace, will you marry me?"

Grace's chin quivered and you could tell she was fighting back tears, but she broke into a wide smile and flung her arms around Matt, then she murmured, "I'd be stupid if I didn't."

Seven

Months

Later

Mr. and Mrs. John Edmund Jones

request the honor of your presence

at the marriage of their daughter

Grace Lillian Jones

to

Matt Andrew Martin

son of

Mr. and Mrs. Stephen Michael Martin,

On Saturday, the fourteenth of April

two thousand and twelve

at five o'clock in the evening

Duke University Chapel

Durham, North Carolina

Reception immediately following the ceremony at the

Washington Duke

Exclusively from G. Gossip:

Matt Martin's Secret Engagement!

- How Martin and sister managed to secretly plan wedding to college student, Grace Jones
- Parents are furious! Father says, "We [Mr. and Mrs. Martin] never permitted such foolishness!"
- Why such a rush to the aisle? Martin comments, "Love can't be pushed aside. And since when are short engagements condemned in Hollywood?"

Exclusively from G. Gossip:

Matt Martin and Grace Jones:
Wedding of the Century!

- How Martin's parents were able to get over their children's misbehavior
- The cake! The star–studded guest list! The ring! The custom made dress! And the *devilish* location!

Epilogue

Love can be described in many different forms. It can be Lilly's love for her newly self purchased Beemer. It can be Lilly's brother Jeff who has a major crush on Grace's maid of honor (albeit she is completely out of his league). It can be Alexa's love for her new boyfriend (and also my cousin) Mark. It can be Magdalene's love for being back on the movie set doing Cole Collins's newly titled movie: *Spontaneous Dating*. It can be my new found love for wedding planning. It can be my parents' love that has now lasted for twenty-five years. Or, of course, it can be my player-turned-doting-gentleman brother Matt's love for his fiancée and "princess" Grace.

Coming soon…the eagerly-awaited sequel to *Finding My Brother's Princess*…

Playing

Fairy Godmother

Rachel Jeffries lives with her two adoring parents in the Valley of the Sun. She loves her big sister, brother-in-law, niece and nephew in the Rocky Mountain State. She loves her grandparents, aunts, uncles and cousins in the United States, Italy and Heaven. She seeks to serve others via Girl Scouts of America, National Junior Honor Society (NJHS), and National Charity League. She is currently a 2nd Degree Black Belt in Taekwondo, and she thanks God for her abundant blessings.

☺ ☺ ☺

Made in the USA
Lexington, KY
09 June 2011